"THE BLUE MAN?"

Thaddeus paused, obviously wondering if the cop was trying to pull a fast one. "I don't remember any Blue Man."

"You don't?" laughed the cop. "Hell, he's the weirdest of the lot!"

"Tojo," said Thaddeus, "stick your head in there and see if we've got a Blue Man."

I walked over to the van. I was too small to peek in the window, so I opened the door while Dave stood beside me, brandishing his pistol. It was dark inside, but I had no trouble seeing the Man of Many Colors. There were four others that I recognized, and then I saw a movement just behind the driver's seat. There was something bluish there, making the same grunting and growling noises I had heard behind the locked door of the sideshow. I caught a glimpse of a satanic countenance much more evil than that of the Horned Demon, and I slammed the door shut. . . .

SIDESHOW

Science Fiction from SIGNET

SIDESHOW

Tales of the
Galactic Midway #1

by
Mike Resnick

A SIGNET BOOK
NEW AMERICAN LIBRARY
TIMES MIRROR

NAL BOOKS ARE AVAILABLE AT QUANTITY DISCOUNTS
WHEN USED TO PROMOTE PRODUCTS OR SERVICES. FOR
INFORMATION PLEASE WRITE TO PREMIUM MARKETING
DIVISION, THE NEW AMERICAN LIBRARY, INC., 1633
BROADWAY, NEW YORK, NEW YORK 10019.

 SIGNET TRADEMARK REG. U.S. PAT. OFF. AND FOREIGN COUNTRIES
REGISTERED TRADEMARK—MARCA REGISTRADA
HECHO EN CHICAGO, U.S.A.

SIGNET, SIGNET CLASSICS, MENTOR, PLUME, MERIDIAN AND NAL
BOOKS *are published by The New American Library, Inc.,*
1633 Broadway, New York, New York 10019

FIRST PRINTING, OCTOBER, 1982

1   2   3   4   5   6   7   8   9

PRINTED IN THE UNITED STATES OF AMERICA

To Carol, as always,
And to Sheila Gilbert,
one of that diminishing group of editors with
convictions—and the courage of them.

1.

The Dog-Faced Boy made me want to cry and run for an exit, both at the same time.

He had the same kind of foreshortened head that you see on a bulldog or a pug, with huge furrows of loose skin wrinkling down from his forehead, and a jaw that took up the bottom half of his face. His nose didn't look like a dog's—it wasn't black or leathery or anything—but the nostrils were set farther apart than any I've ever seen, as if he'd run face-first into a brick wall at full speed and had never bothered to have the cartilage fixed. His ears were tiny little things; you got the feeling that he couldn't hear anything softer than a rifle shot.

But it was his eyes that fascinated me. They were dark brown, and hauntingly sad: old eyes, too old for the rest of his face, eyes that would never be shocked or scared or amused again. And, like a dog's eyes, they had haws: thin membranes that formed an inner eyelid for keeping the wind and dirt out.

I couldn't imagine how he could look at that face in a mirror and still want to go on living. It frightened and repelled me, even as it aroused a wave of pity for its owner.

"Not bad," said Thaddeus, lighting a cigarette and blowing the smoke toward the Dog-Faced Boy. "Not bad at all."

"It's horrible," I said.

"But effective," Thaddeus replied. "I wonder what he sounds like."

As if on cue, the Dog-Faced Boy emitted a trio of piercing barks that sounded more like a seal than a canine.

"Very impressive," said Thaddeus. "Remind me to have a little talk with Elmer when we get back."

Elmer—aided by three hours of makeup and two years' experience in summer stock—was our own Dog-Faced Boy.

Thaddeus blew another mouthful of smoke at the Dog-Faced Boy, got no reaction, and walked to the next booth to look at the Human Lizard.

The Human Lizard was naked except for a pair of shorts. He sat on a small wooden chair atop a raised platform, his back rigid, his hands braced against his knees, staring unblinkingly at us. It was impossible to tell what his expression was like, for his face—like his entire body—was covered by scales. Not leprous sores that gave the illusion of a snakelike texture, not the permanent skin condition that so many Lizard Men have, but sleek, shiny reptilian scales that played with the light the way a prism does. His skin looked moist and oiled, and rippled over his muscles like some living fabric, vaguely greenish in hue. He was devoid of any bodily hair, and when I was finally able to start picking out his facial features I decided that I didn't like them: his eyes looked too cold and dead, and his jaw was set very strangely onto his head.

"I don't like it here, Thaddeus," I said. "Let's go home."

"Shut up," said Thaddeus, never taking his eyes off the Human Lizard. "Do you see a zipper anywhere?"

"A zipper?" I repeated. "Thaddeus, that's not a costume!"

"I didn't see one either," he said grimly. "Damn!"

We stopped next at the Three-Breasted Woman. She had a veil wrapped around her, but when she saw us approaching she let it slide down to the floor. She was wearing sort of a harem or belly-dancing costume—you know, big puffy translucent pants with ankle bracelets and a jingly belt. All three breasts were bare except for a trio of sequined pasties. Each pasty had a tassel hanging down from it, and she put her hands behind her head and started rotating her hips and shoulders until all three tassels were whirling like tiny helicopter propellers.

I turned beet-red and lowered my eyes. That must have amused her, because she started laughing at me. Then she began doing some gyrations that were designed to shock Thaddeus. I could have told her to save her energy: nothing shocks Thaddeus. He watched her for a few minutes, then walked after me.

"Sweat on all three of them," he said. "No wonder we're losing business."

2

We walked past the Missing Link and the Human Pincushion and the Man of Many Colors and the Cyclops, and finally stopped in front of the India Rubber Man. He smiled at us, stood up, stretched his body an extra twelve or thirteen inches, and then bent his arms and legs and fingers in every possible direction, and a couple of impossible ones as well. Two of the children in the crowd started screaming, and I thought for a minute that one of the women was going to faint.

Suddenly a tall, lean man with piercing eyes and an aquiline nose stepped out from behind a curtain. He was wearing a candy-striped jacket and a straw boater, both of which appeared terribly out of place on him; he looked as if he'd be more at home in a floor-length black robe, or at least the kind of cape you see in bad Dracula movies.

"I trust you've all enjoyed the Ahasuerus Traveling Sideshow," he said in English that was almost too perfect. "If anyone feels our advertising has been in any way fraudulent, or that our exhibits are not what they were represented to be, I shall be more than happy to refund your money."

He looked like he didn't expect any takers, and he wasn't disappointed. Most of the crowd filed out in silence.

"Are you Mr. Ahasuerus?" asked Thaddeus, walking up to him. He was one of the few people Thaddeus couldn't meet at eye level.

"I am privileged to work for him," said the tall man. "My name is Romany."

"Well, Mr. Romany," said Thaddeus, extending his hand, "I wonder if it might be possible for me to have a couple of words in private with Mr. Ahasuerus?"

"I'm afraid it's completely out of the question, Mr. Flint," said Mr. Romany, staring at Thaddeus' outstretched hand.

"How did you know my name?" asked Thaddeus.

"Oh, we've been expecting you for quite some time now."

"Just scouting out the opposition," said Thaddeus. "You've got yourself a hell of a freak show."

"We prefer to call them Nature's Wonders," said Mr. Romany disapprovingly. " 'Freaks' is such an ugly word, don't you think?"

3

"Oh, I don't know," said Thaddeus. "I've always believed in calling a spade a spade." He looked down at me. "What do *you* think, Tojo?"

"It's a demeaning word," I said. Or, rather, I *tried* to say it, but I had trouble getting the words out, as usual, and Thaddeus had to translate for me.

"You'll have to forgive my friend," said Thaddeus. "He's one of Nature's Wonders himself."

"I can't help it if I stammer," I managed to say.

"Are you an associate of Mr. Flint's?" asked Mr. Romany.

"He's my bodyguard," said Thaddeus with a smile.

"I see," said Mr. Romany, showing no reaction whatsoever.

There was a long, awkward silence.

"If you've nothing further to say, I have work to do," said Mr. Romany at last. "It has been an honor meeting you."

"Do you mind if we look around a bit more?" asked Thaddeus innocently.

"Be my guest," replied Mr. Romany. His face looked disappointed, but I got the feeling that his eyes were amused. "We do have one rule, however, Mr. Flint: we do not allow spectators to speak to our exhibits."

"You wouldn't be afraid I'll buy a couple of them off, would you?" asked Thaddeus.

"No," said Mr. Romany, and this time there was no doubt that he was amused. "We simply feel that conversing with them would remove some of their air of mystery and, shall we say, novelty."

"Whatever you say," replied Thaddeus.

Mr. Romany walked off without another word, and Thaddeus began walking slowly around the perimeter of the huge tent.

"You see that door that says 'No Admittance'?" he whispered to me.

"Yes," I said.

"What do you suppose is behind it?"

I told him I didn't know, and he chuckled.

"I'll lay you plenty of seven-to-five that it's this Ahasuerus guy's office," he said.

"But Mr. Romany said that he won't speak to anyone," I said.

4

"I'm not just *anyone*," replied Thaddeus. "While I keep Romany busy, why don't you just scoot over there and see where it leads?"

"But—"

"Nobody who wastes as much time reading as you do can hold much truck with ignorance being bliss."

"I don't want any trouble," I said.

"Well," grinned Thaddeus, "you just think about it for a few seconds and see if you can decide who can give you more trouble—Romany or me."

I sighed and began approaching the door as indirectly as I could while Thaddeus walked after Mr. Romany and tried to engage him in conversation. When I finally got there I found that it wasn't just a tent flap, but a solid metal door. I looked around to make sure no one was watching me and tried the handle. It was locked.

Then I put my ear to the door and listened. I couldn't hear any voices, but I heard some strange grunting or growling sound. It wasn't like anything I'd ever heard before, and it scared me. I walked away quickly and caught Thaddeus' eye. He left Mr. Romany and joined me a minute later.

"Well?" he demanded.

"It was locked."

"I knew it! It's got to be Ahasuerus' office."

"I don't think so," I replied. "I heard strange sounds coming from there."

He asked me what kind, and I tried to reproduce them, but I had even more trouble than I have with words, and finally he got tired of listening.

"Well, whatever it is, I want a look inside," he said decisively. "Maybe we'll come back later after he's closed up shop for the day."

"I don't think we should," I said.

"If I listened to you, we'd both be on welfare," he snapped. "This guy's got more freaks than he needs. I've got a bunch of frustrated actors who couldn't draw flies at a watermelon party. We ought to be able to reach an agreement. I want to meet this guy Ahasuerus, feel him out, find out what gets to him."

"As long as it isn't money," I said.

"If I had money, I wouldn't be here trying to make a deal, you goddamned dwarf!" said Thaddeus. "Money

5

can't be the only thing that turns him on, or he wouldn't be out here in the middle of Vermont with a patched-up tent and no heater, playing for quarters and half dollars. Maybe I can interest him in shacking up with one of the girls from the meat show."

"Maybe he won't want to reach that kind of agreement."

"Then maybe I'll trade you to him for the Rubber Man," said Thaddeus irritably. "Just once, I wish you'd stop telling me what I can't do." His eyes fell on the Three-Breasted Woman, and he turned to face her. "Wouldn't *she* go over in the meat show!"

I was going to answer him, but just then she looked right at me and winked and I started blushing furiously, so I just turned away and said nothing.

"Well, there's no reason why this should be a totally wasted trip," said Thaddeus, smiling at the Three-Breasted Woman. "Take a walk, Tojo."

"Where?" I asked.

"Anywhere. I don't want an ugly little wart like you cramping my style."

"Mr. Romany said not to talk to the exhibits."

"And Thaddeus Flint said *scram!*" he snapped.

I could see from the familiar predatory smirk on his face that nothing I could say or do was going to keep him away from the Three-Breasted Woman, so I shrugged and walked out the exit. I knew that Thaddeus wasn't inclined to accept an answer of No from a woman—*any* woman—so I felt I had at least half an hour to kill even if his quest was ultimately unsuccessful.

The cold October wind chilled me right through my coat, and I zipped it all the way to the top. It was twilight, and the crowds were starting to come out in force.

The carnival only had a trio of rides—the Zipper, the Tilt-a-Whirl, and a Ferris wheel—and none of them were doing much business, probably due to the weather. There were about twenty games lining the Midway, and from what I could see most of them were honest. There was also a Bozo-Cage setup—one of those things where you throw balls at a target and try to dunk the guy sitting inside the cage—but the water was too cold, and there was nobody on duty. I couldn't see any signs of a girlie show, even though the local cops were pretty lenient about how

6

strong the girls could work. There were three food stands, which were doing a fair business selling coffee and red-hots, and one of them had also warmed up a huge tureen of soup.

I found it pretty easy to reach the same conclusion as Thaddeus: it was the freak show that was taking all our business away. Our rides were better, our games were more exciting, our girls had no competition, even our food stands were better stocked. Except for the freak show, it was a pretty patched-up and run-of-the-mill carnival, the kind that goes from town to town renting out to local Jaycee groups every weekend.

The freak show made up for the rest of it, though. If there were two thousand people on the grounds, eighteen hundred had to be inside the tent or lined up to buy tickets. Paying money to gape at someone else's deformity was a concept that I could never understand—but then, I could never figure out why happily married men bought tickets to our girlie show, either.

It was totally dark out when I decided to go back and see if Thaddeus was ready to leave yet. As I was walking toward the tent a group of men fell into step behind me. I stepped aside to let them pass, but they came to a stop too.

"What the hell is *he* doing out of the freak show?" said one of them, and the others all laughed.

"Hey, sonny, ain't it past your bedtime?" said another.

I kept my eyes trained on the tent and kept walking. Suddenly a hand reached out and grabbed my shoulder, swinging me around.

"Where's your manners?" said a blond man with long greasy hair and an acne-marked face. "Didn't you hear me just ask you a question?"

I tried to tell him to leave me alone, but I couldn't force the words out.

"What's the matter?" laughed another of the men, and I could see now that there were five of them. "Cat got your tongue?"

I made an attempt to reply, but again nothing came out.

"Why pay money for a freak show when we can look at you for free?" said the blond man.

7

I gave up trying to speak and just glared at him.

"Ugly little bastard, isn't he?" said another.

"Come on," said the blond man. "I'm getting tired of looking at him."

"Maybe he's getting tired of looking at you," said a familiar voice behind me.

"Who the hell are *you*?" said the blond man.

"I'm the guy who's going to make you apologize to my friend," said Thaddeus, stepping between them and me.

"You and what army?" laughed the blond man.

Thaddeus didn't reply. He just stepped forward and hit the blond man full on the jaw, and slammed a fist into another man's stomach before the first one had hit the ground.

"My friend is still waiting for that apology," said Thaddeus, a wicked smile on his face.

The other three jumped him, and I ran off to get a policeman while Thaddeus started cursing and hitting with equal vigor. When I returned with two security guards a minute later three of the men were lying on the ground, while Thaddeus and the other two were still flailing away, blood pouring down their faces.

The guards broke up the fight and decided to settle for ejecting everyone from the grounds rather than making any arrests. They let Thaddeus and me leave first.

"Well," he said as we were driving out of the parking lot, "aren't you going to thank me for saving your ugly little neck?"

"It wasn't necessary," I said. "They were just teasing me. *You* do it all the time."

"I've got a right," he said. "They don't."

"They wouldn't have hurt me," I persisted.

"How the hell do you know?" he shot back. "Besides, I *like* an occasional fight."

"Especially after a woman has turned you down," I said softly.

"I've got to do *something* with all that energy," he agreed. Suddenly he turned to me. "What makes you think she turned me down?" he asked sharply.

"Just a guess," I said.

"Well, if she hadn't, I wouldn't have been around to pull your fat out of the fire," he said petulantly.

"They wouldn't have hurt me," I repeated. "They were about to leave."

"Goddamned ungrateful little dwarf," he muttered. We drove the rest of the way in total silence.

2.

Thaddeus calls me a dwarf, but I'm not.

What I am is a hunchback. He knows it, of course, but he can't make any money displaying a hunchback in a sideshow. He says that people have this regrettable tendency to feel sorry for hunchbacks, rather than being fascinated or scared by them. He doesn't know why, given the splendid example of Quasimodo, but that's the way he says it is. He even tried billing me as the World's Smallest Hunchback—the best of two worlds, he called it—but it didn't work. (Actually, if I could stand erect the way I used to be able to do when I was growing up, I'd probably be five foot three or four: not enormous, but not a dwarf, either.)

He also calls me Tojo: it isn't my name—or, at least, it didn't use to be. But my eyes are kind of narrow, and my hair is black, and my skin has a yellow cast to it from all the times I've been sick. Thaddeus decided the first time he saw me that if my name wasn't Tojo it ought to be—and since I didn't want my parents to find me and send me back to the sanitarium, I figured that Tojo was as good a name as any and better than most. To this day, I don't think Thaddeus knows my real name.

We share a trailer except when Thaddeus has feminine company, which means we don't share a trailer very often at all. The night we came back from the Ahasuerus Traveling Sideshow, Thaddeus picked up one of the local girls, and I spent the night with Jupiter Monk, our wild animal trainer. He's a nice, friendly guy, and one of the few members of the carny who can discuss books with me, but he keeps a pair of leopards in his trailer and I spent most of the night sleeping in his tub with the door locked. Every now and then he'd knock on the door and ask if I needed anything, and when I told him I didn't he'd go back to wrestling with his animals.

Still, it was better than spending a night with some of

10

the others. Jason Diggs—he runs our games and is known, less than lovingly, as Digger the Rigger—won't let me in unless I agree to play cards with him. Even playing for nickels and dimes, a night's rent can get pretty expensive. And Billybuck Dancer, our trick-shot artist, just sits in his chair all night and stares at photographs of Doc Holliday and Johnny Ringo; I think he's a little crazy, even if he is the best gun-and-knife man I've ever seen in a carny.

In fact, thanks to Thaddeus' incredibly complicated love life, I spend two or three nights in every trailer on the lot during the course of a season. Except Alma's, that is.

Alma is Alma Pafko. She's also Honeysuckle Rose, one of the girls in the strip show, although Thaddeus replaced her as the headliner last year. She's also Thaddeus' steady bedmate, although that gets a little complicated, too. She knows that he sleeps with other women in the show, and while I know it bothers her she puts up with it; but she goes crazy when he picks up one of the locals. She loves him, and she won't sleep with anyone else, but she realizes that he has his faults, so in her mind she's drawn an imaginary line around the carny: as long as he keeps it in the family, so to speak, she tolerates it.

Alma and I used to be friends. In fact, for a long time she was my only friend. She would take care of me when I got sick, and she'd stick up for me whenever Thaddeus started picking on me, and she even set up a kind of screen so that I wouldn't have to leave the trailer on cold nights. I used to lend her books, and while she was never really interested in them, at least she'd make an effort to read them. We even traded Christmas presents.

We would spend long afternoons sitting around the trailer discussing the future. Alma was always going to quit the girlie show, though of course she never did. I don't think she felt especially degraded by stripping, but it always bothered her when Thaddeus would pass the word that the cops were in the bag and the girls could work strong. She didn't mind the men pawing and kissing her, but it upset the hell out of her that *he* didn't mind it either.

She kept talking about wanting to become a legitimate actress on the New York stage (unless, of course, she could talk Thaddeus into marrying her, which was what she *really* wanted). I don't think she had ever seen a live play in her life, but I don't imagine it was any sillier than my own ambition: from the day I first saw Thaddeus standing on a platform in front of the girlie show, taunting and joking with his audience, teasing and prodding them into buying tickets and out-heckling the hecklers, I'd wanted to be a barker for a carny. I even sent off for a couple of speech-improvement courses, but they didn't improve my stammer any more than the Albee and Williams plays I loaned to Alma improved her acting.

Still, it was nice to sit around and dream, and we did a lot of it—until the day Thaddeus got an opportunity to buy out Jonas Stark, the carny's owner. He begged and borrowed and connived and conned for the down payment, and still came up a couple of thousand dollars short. It looked like the deal was going to fall apart, and then one day he walked into the trailer while Alma and I were sitting there talking to each other and announced that he had found a way to get his hands on the rest of the money.

It turned out that one of the locals had attended the girlie show every night for two weeks, and had a real thing about Alma. He'd heard Thaddeus trying to round up the money, and had offered to make up the difference in exchange for a little something "special." That something turned out to be a privately made film produced expressly for him. He wanted to watch Alma having sex with one of the freaks from the sideshow, but since they were just a bunch of actors in makeup, Thaddeus had decided to use me, since according to him I was the closest thing we had to a real freak.

We both objected, but Thaddeus hit the roof, screaming that there was a time limit on raising the money and that so far neither of us had contributed a red cent, that he had been carrying us for months. I expected Alma to walk out on him then, but she just sat very still and told him to get his camera, and when it was set up she began doing her standard strip for it.

Then Thaddeus aimed the lens at me, and I started shaking like a leaf. I had never had a woman before, and I was scared to death—and besides, this wasn't just *any* woman. It was Alma, and it made me feel cheap and dirty.

Thaddeus begged and pleaded and taunted and cajoled me, just the way he did with marks on the Midway, a parallel that wasn't lost on any of us. I looked at Alma lying back on the bed, totally nude, her face an expressionless mask, her legs spread apart, her clitoris glistening like a moist pearl in its blond velvet setting, tears trickling down her cheek, and I began crying too. I had dreamed of someday making love to a woman—even fumblemouthed hunchbacks can dream—but never like this. I had never been farther from having an erection in my life, but then Thaddeus directed Alma to do certain things to me, and almost against my will I was suddenly able to perform. I felt her shudder—with disgust? Who knows—as I lay on top of her and her arms encircled me and came in contact with my hump, I saw our tears mingling as they rolled down her face and onto her neck, I sensed her muscles fighting against the urge to get up and run from the trailer, and finally it was over and Thaddeus got his money and owned his carnival. I've never been with a woman again.

It was weeks before Alma and I could even nod hello to each other. We've never sat down and spoken again the way we used to—oh, we exchange information when we have to, but we never talk about our hopes and dreams and fears anymore—and of all the things Thaddeus has done, that is the one I've never forgiven him for. He cost me a friend, and nobody has so many friends that they can afford to lose one. Especially not me.

Alma and I stayed with the carnival even after Thaddeus took it over. I had nowhere else to go, and impossible as it may sound, she still loved him. I don't think she *liked* him anymore, but evidently she could differentiate between the two. And after a while, our wounds healed, even if the memories remained.

Thaddeus wasted no time assembling our rather odd crew. He recruited old Stogie—an aging baggy-pants comic whose real name was Max Bloom and who hadn't worked in perhaps twenty years—to work the girlie show in the evenings so the girls would have a few minutes to rest between performances. Stogie specialized in jokes that were so old that even *Captain Billy's Whiz Bang*

13

hadn't bothered with them half a century ago; on the other hand, as Thaddeus was fond of confiding to me, he was too damned old and feeble to present any competition with the girls. As for Alma and the rest, they appreciated the brief respite from leering old men. (There was nothing altruistic about it, of course; Thaddeus just didn't think they pulled in as much money when they looked tired, but since it worked out well all the way around no one objected to his motivation.) If Stogie ever drew a laugh I never heard it, but I suppose he served much the same purpose as I did: people looked at me or listened to him, and suddenly they were a little more content with the way they were.

After a couple of the girls got attacked while working as strong as Thaddeus wanted them to, he decided to get a roughie for the show. Real bouncers cost too much, so he picked up a former pro football lineman named Big Alvin. (I never found out his last name, though I suppose it's in the record books somewhere.) Big Alvin was a big pussycat—he quit football because he didn't like hurting opposing players—but he looked like the Hulk, and when the rowdies saw him they didn't misbehave long enough to find out if he'd actually throw them out. The smart money around the carny said that he wouldn't lift a finger to save anyone, but fortunately the situation never arose.

Thaddeus even hired a former strip star from the heyday of burlesque, Joannie Pym, to act as a kind of den mother for the girls. Her official title, for reasons I'm still not totally clear about, was Queen Bee. Everyone called her Queenie, and her job, as near as I could tell, was to see to it that the girls didn't go to bed with anyone except Thaddeus. Outside of that, she worked on their costumes (since most of them started out naked, there wasn't an awful lot of work involved) and sobered them up when they needed it, which was almost every night.

Thaddeus always wanted a freak show. Jonas Stark had thought they were perverted and unnatural, so when Thaddeus took over the carnival he had to put one together from scratch. The only legitimate freak he ever got was Merrymax, an honest-to-God hermaphrodite. No matter how hard he looked, he never came up with a second one, which was one of the reasons he was so sensitive about the Ahasuerus Traveling Sideshow. He tried displaying me for a couple of nights, but no one was impressed. He hired a guy called Bill Koonce, who stood seven feet ten and was once offered a tryout with the New York Knicks; he dubbed him Treetop and even bought him a pair of elevator shoes, but after a week Treetop was setting up tents and stands on the Midway like everyone else. The one person besides Merrymax who stuck was Little Lulu, a forty-two-inch midget whose real name was Lulu Toole. I think Thaddeus kept her around for my benefit, but nothing ever happened: I found her appallingly unattractive, and she used to get furious trying to understand what I was saying. The only other oddity we carried was Hunkie, our geek. I don't know his name either—in point of fact, we had had four different Hunkies before the current one—but it was rumored that he used to be a newspaper writer before he developed a taste for sniffing coke and biting off chickens' heads.

When he finally realized that he wasn't going to be able to round up a batch of "real" freaks, Thaddeus started hiring fake ones. Maybe because he himself was so drawn to the odd and the bizarre, he was absolutely convinced there were enormous profits to be made from a freak show, and he kept trying—unsuccessfully—to put one together.

Anyway, Digger the Rigger kept us above water— barely—for the first year, and the strip show contributed a little, and then somewhere along the way Thaddeus picked up Billybuck Dancer. The Dancer is the most polite, soft-spoken guy you'd ever want to meet—he always stands when a woman enters the room, always tips his hat and even calls the strippers "ma'am" in his lilting Texas drawl, never drinks or smokes—but like I said, he's a little bit crazy. There was even a story making the rounds that he once won a shootout with a famous Argentinean outlaw. As the story goes, they rented out a huge soccer arena in Buenos Aires and sold tickets. I don't know if it's true, but I see no reason why it shouldn't be. At any rate, the Dancer is an exciting entertainer: he's a crack shot—Thaddeus made me his assistant for a month, so I can vouch for it—and he's so handsome that all the girls pay to see him while their husbands and boyfriends are watching the strip show. He's a sad man, always giving the impression that he wishes he

15

were somewhere else, or maybe some*time* else. One thing I know: He's the only man on the lot that Thaddeus has never picked a fight with.

And then there's Jupiter Monk. After the Dancer started drawing crowds, Thaddeus decided that we needed another specialty act. I don't know where he heard about Monk, but he sent for him, and one day Monk appeared on our doorstep, a huge burly man with a drooping handlebar mustache, dressed like some wild Russian Cossack and accompanied by a bear, a lion, and two leopards. He's good at his trade, I suppose, but I think he'd be even better working the games: he's the only person the Rigger has never been able to beat at cards or craps. (Or maybe the Rigger loses on purpose: I know *I* sure wouldn't want a lion tamer mad at me.)

For a while we had a sword swallower, too. He called himself Carlos the Magnificent, though his real name was Julian Levy, and he drew pretty good crowds until the night he showed up drunk and practically gutted himself.

About a year ago Thaddeus decided that Alma wasn't putting her heart into her work (it took him that long to notice), so he sent off to a strippers' school—they really do have one, out in California somewhere—and hired Gloria Stunkel, a gorgeous young girl who dances under the name of Butterfly Delight. He moved her into the headliner's spot the day she arrived; I think Alma was actually happy about it, since the star is supposed to work even stronger than the other girls. But Gloria turned out to be a double oddity in the strip show: she wouldn't work strong, and she wouldn't go to bed with Thaddeus. The customers never liked her, since they weren't paying for an artful striptease, but Thaddeus kept her around anyway, either because she amused him or because she presented a challenge, I'm still not sure which.

We were a motley crew, all right, but we got along pretty well together, especially when Thaddeus wasn't around. I can't say I was truly happy with the carnival, but I know that I was less unhappy than I'd been anywhere else. Thaddeus may have treated me like dirt—but he treated me like *normal* dirt, a little on the stupid side because of my stammer, but nothing to be fussed over. And if he displayed a certain disregard of my feelings, well, he behaved no differently toward anyone else. After a lifetime of being patronized, you can't imagine what that meant to me.

I was sitting down at a wooden table near one of the concession stands the morning after we had been to see Mr. Ahasuerus' show, drinking some coffee and trying to keep warm, when Queenie and Alma walked over and sat down across from me. Alma sat a little distance away, like she always does, but Queenie leaned forward until her face was maybe ten inches away from mine.

"I hear you went with him last night," she said.

"That's right," I replied.

"To see this freak show that everyone's talking about?"

I nodded.

She pulled a small flask of whiskey out of her coat pocket and took a swig, then offered some to Alma.

"No, thank you," said Alma, not looking at either of us.

"Come on, honey, it'll keep you warm," said Queenie, throwing an arm around Alma's shoulders. Alma just shook her head and edged away, and I could see that Queenie didn't like that any more than Alma liked having a woman's arm around her.

"Was it any good?" demanded Queenie.

It took me a minute to figure out that she was talking to me.

"Was what any good?" I asked.

"The freak show, you demented little toad!" snapped Queenie. "What the hell have we been talking about?"

"It was good," I said.

"As good as they say?"

"Yes."

"Shit!" she said. "He's going to get his hands on it, isn't he?"

I brushed away a couple of leaves that had blown onto the table next to my coffee cup. "I don't think it's for sale," I said.

"Who said anything about buying it? You ought to know him by now. He's going to take it over one way or another, and then we'll all be out in the cold."

"He won't do that, Queenie," I said.

"You think he likes you!" snorted Queenie. "This stupid little bitch"—she gestured to Alma—"thinks he loves her. Well, let me tell you: he doesn't like or love anyone.

17

He *uses* you, just like he uses everyone else around here."

Alma kind of flinched when she said that.

"It's not true," I said. "I know he loves Alma." Not only didn't I know it, but it was hard to sound soothing and confident at a rate of six words a minute. Still, I tried.

"Oh, shut up, Tojo!" said Alma, still not looking at me.

I wanted to reach out and touch her hand, to do something to comfort her, but I didn't know what to do, so I just sat still.

"You don't love someone and treat her the way he treats Alma," said Queenie. There was a look on her face that implied *she'd* know how to treat someone she loved.

"Even if that's true," I said at last, "even if he cuts everyone loose, that wouldn't be so terrible, would it, Alma? After all, you've wanted to quit for years."

She finally looked at me. "I'm twenty-nine years old," she said bitterly, "and the only thing I know how to do is walk out naked on a stage and let a bunch of strange men paw my body."

"I thought you wanted to be an actress," I said. I knew it was a stupid thing to say, but I couldn't think of anything else.

"You think someone's going to put up a million dollars just so I can play Blanche Du Bois on Broadway?" she said with a self-deprecating little laugh. "Look at what I am, Tojo. Who would have me?"

"There, there, baby," said Queenie, putting her arm around Alma's shoulders again, and this time Alma didn't move away. "You see what you've done?" said Queenie, turning to me. "You've got her crying now."

"I didn't mean to," I said.

"It's *him*," said Queenie, which was her way of accepting my apology. "We hang around him long enough and suddenly we start acting like him."

I didn't think I was acting like Thaddeus, but I didn't reply.

"You let us know what's going on with that freak show," said Queenie, getting up and helping Alma to her feet. "You keep us informed of the situation, okay?"

I nodded.

Alma walked a few yards away with Queenie and then turned back to me, her eyes filling with tears. "Why do we stay here, Tojo?" she asked plaintively. "Why do we let him do these things to us?"

"I don't know," I said.

It was a lie. All you had to do was look around to know why: at the Dancer, who was born a century too late; at Monk, who loved his animals more than he loved women; at the Rigger, who couldn't play an honest game of anything if his life depended on it; at the girls, who pretended that they were dancers and entertainers; at Stogie, who still thought he was in vaudeville; at me; at Queenie; at any of us.

We are *all* freaks. Like deserters hiding out in the middle of a battlefield, we seek the anonymity of the spotlight. The world turns a cold shoulder toward us, and we huddle together for warmth.

3.

It was noon when Thaddeus stuck his head out the trailer window and hollered for me. The sun had come out, and while the air was still crisp, it was a lot warmer than when I had spoken with Alma and Queenie a few hours earlier.

"Coming!" I muttered, getting up from the picnic table and shuffling over to the trailer. I slipped once as I was clambering up the four steps—I usually do—and skinned the heel of my left hand.

Thaddeus was sitting on the side of his bed, totally naked, holding his head in his hands and trying to keep the light out of his eyes. There was a young girl I didn't recognize, sound asleep and equally naked, lying next to him.

"Coffee!" he rasped.

I went off to the kitchen and put the pot on, then returned to him. Thaddeus sat motionless for another minute, then slowly began getting into his shorts.

"She's awfully young," I said.

He looked over at the girl. "She wants to work in the meat show," he said with a laugh. "She'll never know how lucky she is that I don't hire everyone I sleep with. Hell, if she's as much as seventeen, I'm Whistler's Mother. You'd think her parents would keep closer tabs on her." He paused, then sighed. "Slip twenty bucks into her purse and get her out of here."

"Did it ever occur to you that she might consider that degrading?" I said.

"You really think so?" He looked surprised.

"Yes, I do."

"How else do you thank a kid her age? Buy her a doll?" He looked at her again, then shrugged and flashed me a sardonic smile. "I defer to your vast experience with women. Keep the money and get rid of her."

"In a few minutes," I said. "I saw Alma outside."

"So what?" he said ominously.

"Well, I just think you should wait until she's out of sight before—"

"Since when is what goes on between Alma and me any of your business?" he said hotly. "She never minded when people saw *her* leaving here. She knows I don't sleep alone."

"But this girl is a local. She's not one of us."

"That's Alma's hang-up, not mine."

"But you don't have to flaunt—"

"I seem to recall asking for coffee," he said. "I don't remember requesting a sermon."

I sighed, returned to the kitchen, and spent a couple of minutes washing some dirty dishes I found in the sink. When the coffee was ready I poured him a big cup—black, no sugar—and took it over to him. He was totally dressed, and he grabbed the coffee from me, took a long swallow, and handed back the empty cup.

"More," he said.

I filled it up again, and when I got back he was standing next to the bed, looking at the girl. He reached down and poked her gently on the shoulder. "Come on, babe—up and at 'em."

She yawned, stretched once or twice, and then sat up, rubbing her eyes. Then she saw me, and she shrieked and pulled the covers up over her small breasts.

"What the hell is *that?*" she yelled.

"My business manager," said Thaddeus, taking the cup from me and draining it again. "He'll walk you home."

"Like hell he will!" she said, shrinking back against the wall of the trailer. "You!" she snapped at me. "Yes, you! Turn your back until I get dressed, and don't you dare come near me!"

I shrugged and walked back into the kitchen.

"But we're partners, honey," I heard Thaddeus saying to her. "We share everything, if you get my meaning."

"If that little monster so much as lays a finger on me, I'll have my father and brothers down here so fast it'll make your head spin!"

I heard a bunch of rustling noises, and then the door slammed and Thaddeus told me I could come back into the bedroom.

21

"How many times have I asked you not to embarrass me like that?" I said.

"It's the quickest way I know to get rid of them," he replied with a little smile. "Besides, who knows—maybe one of these days one of 'em will go for the idea." He looked out the window and blinked. "Nice day. What time is it?"

"Almost twelve-thirty," I said.

"Did we make any money last night?"

"Not much, according to Diggs."

"Figures. Speaking of our friend the Rigger, why don't you run off and find him and bring him back here?" said Thaddeus. "I've got a little job for him."

"Does it have something to do with the sideshow?" I asked suspiciously.

"Nosy little dwarf, aren't you?" he grinned. "Yes, as a matter of fact, it does."

"Surely you don't think you're going to be able to get Mr. Romany or Mr. Ahasuerus in a card game with Diggs?"

"No," replied Thaddeus. "Romany didn't look like the gambling type to me."

"Then what?"

"Why don't you just keep reading your poetry books and let me do the thinking around here?"

He walked into the bathroom and started shaving, so I headed off in search of Digger the Rigger. He was an easy man to pick out in a crowd: close-cropped snow-white hair, neatly manicured goatee, dapper dresser, fingers covered with diamonds, shoes usually shining brighter than the sun. And since the Midway was never crowded at noontime on a weekday, I hunted him up inside of five minutes.

He was standing in front of the specialty tent, trying to make a bet with a couple of earlybird customers about whether Billybuck Dancer could shoot the head off the king of spades at fifty feet. (I knew that he could: I had to hold it between my teeth the time I worked with him, much to Thaddeus' amusement.) The Rigger was really upset with me when I broke into his pitch and the marks wandered away. He probably couldn't have gotten them to put up more than a dollar apiece, but the amount was

22

never as important to him as the game. Anyway, he bitched at me all the way back to the trailer.

"You want to see me?" he said as Thaddeus greeted us.

"How's your poker?" asked Thaddeus. He had made the trailer a little neater than usual, which wasn't saying much, and had pulled a trio of bargain-basement chairs around the aging coffee table where he made out the paychecks (on those weeks he could meet the payroll).

"You had the dwarf drag me all the way over here just to ask a stupid question like that?" snorted the Rigger.

"If I'm going to stake you," said Thaddeus, "I think the least you can do is answer my question."

"Let me get this straight," said the Rigger slowly. "*You're* staking *me?*"

Thaddeus smiled. "That's right."

"My poker's the same as it always is."

"You'll be playing with someone else's cards," said Thaddeus.

"What do I care?"

"They're probably marked."

"There ain't a marked deck in the world that I can't read as well as the owner can," said the Rigger with just a trace of pride.

"You're sure?" said Thaddeus. "Eight hundred dollars is everything I've got in the world, as of this minute. I don't want to turn it over to you if you've got any doubts."

"No sweat," said the Rigger, but he looked a little more serious now, a little more tense—or perhaps he was just a little more eager. "Are these people I'm playing with any good?"

"*They* think they are."

"What makes you think they'll use a trick deck?"

"They confiscate them all the time," chuckled Thaddeus. "They're cops."

"You think I'm just going to walk into a police station, sit down at a table, and scare up a friendly little game?" asked the Rigger.

"I set it up last night," said Thaddeus.

"With cops?" repeated the Rigger unbelievingly.

"With cops."

"If I win, they'll shut us down and arrest half the girls."

"No they won't," said Thaddeus. "First of all, they're

23

already in the bag on the meat show. And second, I don't want their money."

"Let me get this straight: you're staking me to eight hundred dollars, and you don't want their money. Have I got that right so far?"

"Yes."

"What *do* you want?"

"Their markers," said Thaddeus. "You play them for cash, they'll quit when they run out. Play them for their markers, and they just might drop a bundle. Lose a few hundred at the start, though, just to give them a little confidence."

"I still don't understand. Cops don't have that much money, so what good are their markers?"

"Oh, I'll think of some way to redeem them," said Thaddeus, and suddenly I knew what he planned to do. He turned to me. "You stick with him, Tojo, and keep an eye on my money. I want it all back—minus a hundred for the Rigger's time, that is."

I followed Diggs to the Hothouse—the heated tent that's open from noon to midnight for the crew to take their breaks—and watched him spend the next three hours preparing for the game at an empty table. First he went through some exercises to warm up his fingers. Then he broke out three new decks, placed them in front of him, and began shuffling them. He kept at it for about five minutes, then started turning each deck over one card at a time: somehow or other, he had put every suit in numerical order in all three decks.

"Nothing to it," he laughed, when he saw the expression on my face.

"They're marked," I said, though I didn't really believe it.

He shook his head, and started shuffling one of the decks again. "Tell me what hand you want."

"Anything at all?" I asked.

"You name it."

"Four aces."

He shuffled another twenty seconds, then dealt us each five cards face down. I picked my hand up and looked at it: there were four aces, plus a queen of spades. I turned them face up with an exclamation of astonishment.

24

"Pretty good hand," commented the Rigger. "Want to put a little money on it?"

"No. I don't bet."

"Pity," he said, and turned his own hand over. It was a straight flush in clubs, from the seven to the jack.

He laughed heartily, then decided my education had been sadly lacking and showed me the riffle stack, and how to deal seconds and middles. I tried to do it the way he did, but I'm not very coordinated, and it didn't work very well. Then he explained how arm-pressure holdouts worked, and the principles of false carding, and finally he took a double-edged blade out of his wallet and demonstrated the fine arts of line work, edge work, and belly stripping.

"It's fascinating," I said when he was through. "But don't you ever play fair?"

"Bite your tongue, boy," he said with arched eyebrows. "If old Phineas T. could hear that, he'd start spinning nonstop in his grave."

"But putting you in a game against a normal man is like taking candy from a baby."

"Tojo," he said, "if God didn't want them fleeced, He wouldn't have made them sheep. You don't object to rigging the games on the Midway, do you?"

"But that's just for quarters," I said. "You're going to be playing for big money tonight."

"You mean it's okay to cheat them for pennies, but not for dollars?"

It occurred to me that that was exactly what I meant, so I stopped and thought about it for a while. There was a time when I thought any cheating was immoral; now I was hard pressed to find a philosophic justification not to cheat for high stakes as well as low. I guess that's what being around Thaddeus does to a person.

We left the carnival at twilight and arrived at the police station just after dark. They were waiting for us, and they had a table and some chairs set up in an empty cell.

Diggs played them as skillfully as Isaac Stern plays a violin. He won the first hand, then lost six straight and started complaining about his luck. He broke even for the next hour, while one cop started losing to the other two, then struck like a cobra and wiped the low man out.

He never suggested markers, but simply let the cop

watch for a bit while he lost three more hands, then offered to loan him some money. He started drinking and slurring his words, loosening them up and lowering their guards, then managed to pull a full house against a straight and two flushes. That wiped two of them out, and again he offered to loan them some of his winnings. He counted out the money so drunkenly they must have thought he was finally ripe for the picking—and sure enough, they each won a moderate pot before he came up with four nines in a stud game to beat four threes and a full house.

It went on like that for another hour, and then he passed out cold. The game was obviously over, and I totaled up their IOUs: it came to just under sixteen thousand dollars.

Suddenly they realized the full extent of their losses, and I told them not to worry, that I was sure something could be worked out. They went for it like fish for a baited hook, and I told them to meet Thaddeus in his trailer in an hour. Then I had them help me carry the Rigger out to the car.

Fortunately none of them thought to ask how I was going to drive him home, since I needed a specially made seat and controls—and a minute after they left us Diggs sat up, chuckling softly and stone cold sober, and moved into the driver's seat.

"Don't you feel sorry for them?" I asked as we sped back to the carnival.

"A tiger doesn't live long if he starts feeling sorry for his prey, boy," he said, still smiling. "Besides," he added, "do you think they'd have felt sorry for me if I was as drunk as they thought I was and they had cleaned me out?"

"Two wrongs don't make a right," I said.

"True," he agreed. "That's why it's so important to become a skillful wrongdoer—so nobody can wrong you back."

"Do you ever lose?"

"Just against that big lion tamer."

"Why him?"

"He's a patient man," said Diggs. "It takes a lot of patience to work with those killer cats, and it carries over into his other habits. He's used to working with dangerous

26

animals—and that's exactly what I am with a deck of cards, boy: a dangerous animal. He watches me, he studies me, he never makes a move until he's ready."

"But you're more skilled than he is."

"Sometimes that's not enough. Those cats are stronger than he is, but he wins, doesn't he?"

"I've never seen you play Thaddeus," I said. "Could you beat him?"

"Thaddeus would never play me," said the Rigger. "In case it's slipped your notice, Thaddeus doesn't indulge in anything that he can't win." He paused. "Might do him a world of good to get taken to the cleaners at something one of these days. Take a little of the edge off him." He paused again, then shook his head. "Not very damned likely, though, is it?"

I thought of the scene to come, and agreed that it wasn't likely at all.

4.

The morning was cold and windy, with just a trace of snow in the air. Most of the leaves had blown down from the trees during the night, and were swirling across the ground, forming red-gold patterns in the early-morning sun.

Thaddeus had met with the three cops in private the night before. As soon as they left his trailer, he sent out the order to break the booths and the girlie show down and pack them onto our trucks. I thought maybe he'd gone too far with the cops and that they had run him out of town, but then he made a couple of phone calls and sold all the rides, even the Ferris wheel, where they stood. Then I knew he'd gotten what he wanted; otherwise, he'd never have left the rides behind. Getting rid of them made us a lot more mobile—and I had a feeling that whatever deal Thaddeus had struck, mobility was going to be an important part of our immediate future.

We left at daybreak and drove about ten miles out of town. I had no doubt that we were going to a prearranged meeting point, since Thaddeus kept referring to a map he had scribbled on the back of a paper towel. Finally we turned off the road near an abandoned New England farmhouse and pulled up to an unpainted barn. Thaddeus got out, told Jupiter to bring his animal trailer—a converted Greyhound bus, with twenty-four built-in cages—up alongside of us, and then told the Rigger to circle around and lead all the other vehicles to a rendezvous point about five miles up the road.

Then he climbed back into the trailer and waited, while I kept looking out toward the road and Monk tended to his four animals. Five minutes passed, then ten, and no one showed up.

"You're sure they're coming?" I said at last.

He nodded. "They're coming, all right. They may be having a little trouble with Romany and Ahasuerus, but they'll be here." He looked down at his wristwatch, sighed, and leaned back.

Another twenty minutes passed, and then suddenly two police vans turned off the road and pulled up next to us. The three cops who had been in the card game got out, and Thaddeus walked over to greet them.

"Everything under control?" he asked pleasantly, buttoning his leather overcoat and turning up the collar.

"Yes, sir, Mr. Flint," said one of the cops. I think his name was Joe; at least, that's what I'm going to call him.

"Romany give you any trouble?"

"Some," said Joe with a laugh.

Thaddeus paused to watch a flock of southbound geese pass overhead. "How about Ahasuerus?" he asked at last.

"The guy never showed."

Thaddeus looked surprised. "Even after you arrested Romany?"

"That's right, Mr. Flint."

"You made sure Romany knew that I was going to take over all the freaks unless Ahasuerus wanted to talk deal?"

"Absolutely," said Joe.

"How long can you hold him?"

"Well, now, that's kind of strange, Mr. Flint," said Joe. "If you'd asked me two hours ago, I'd have said we might hold him half a day before he got sprung, enough time for you to move out of here and not a hell of a lot more. But we offered to let him make a call to his lawyer, and he turned us down."

"What does that mean?" asked Thaddeus sharply.

"It means he's in for seventy-two or ninety-six hours, depending on when his case comes up."

"And then?"

"Well, we haven't really got anything on him: just a couple of charges about his license not being in order, and maybe something about the way he treated his freaks." Joe paused and shot a quick sideways glance at the two vans. "Have you taken a good look at those things, Mr. Flint? I've seen my share of freak shows like yours before, but I never saw anything like them. I tell you, they're weird!"

"Getting back to Romany," said Thaddeus. "You're sure you can hold him for three days?"

"At least," said Joe. "Who knows? We might even stretch it out to a week if he's too dumb to ask for counsel."

"Okay," said Thaddeus, producing the three IOUs and handing them back to the cops. "You did your part; I'm doing mine."

"Thank you, Mr. Flint," said Joe, checking his IOU and tearing it up. The other cops did the same. "Now, about the other part of our deal."

"Right," said Thaddeus, pulling out the thickest wad of hundred-dollar bills I ever saw in my life. "A thousand apiece, wasn't it?"

"That was the agreement," nodded one of the other cops, eyeing the sheaf of bills hungrily.

"Whose money is that?" I demanded.

"Mine," said Thaddeus. "Whose did you think it was?"

"But you told me you only had eight hundred dollars!" I said.

"I lied to you," he replied, looking amused. "It wasn't the first time I've ever lied; I think you can be reasonably sure it won't be the last."

"And you're using it to *buy* the freaks?" I persisted.

"Look, Shorty," said Joe, "nobody's buying nothing. Romany is in jail, Ahasuerus has flown the coop, and no one else at that carnival knows what the hell's going on. These poor monsters would starve if they had to stay there. We're doing 'em a favor."

I got so mad I couldn't force any words out.

"Calm down, Half-Pint," said another of the cops. "A town like ours ain't got any use for a bunch of freaks. There's a hell of a big difference between gawking at them in a sideshow and supporting them when the show goes under. Now Mr. Flint here has generously agreed to take them with him. He makes a little money, so he's happy; we get a fee for our services and stop them from becoming wards of the state, so we're happy; they get the care and attention they need, and get to do the only kind of work they're cut out for, so they're the happiest of all."

"It works out fine all the way around," said Joe, grinning down at me. "Looks to me like everybody's happy except you."

"Oh, he'll be happy soon enough," said Thaddeus. "It just takes him a while to adjust to new ideas." He gave

30

me a friendly pat on the shoulder, just hard enough to warn me not to say anything further. "Are you ready to transfer them now?"

"Uh . . . I hate to bring up crass financial matters," said Joe, "but there's a little matter of twelve thousand dollars, Mr. Flint."

"I only counted eleven when I was there," said Thaddeus. "You wouldn't be trying to charge me for Tojo here, would you?"

"No, sir, Mr. Flint. Dave, hand me the list." The cop named Dave dug into a pocket and pulled out a crumpled piece of paper. "Well, let's see what we got here," said Joe, squinting at the paper. "The Man of Many Colors, the Cyclops, the Dog-Faced Boy, the Three-Breasted Woman. That's four. The Rubber Man and the Human Lizard. That's six. The Pincushion, the Missing Link, and the Elephant Woman. That's nine. The Blue Man, the Horned Demon, and the Sphinx. That's an even dozen."

"Blue Man?" repeated Thaddeus. "I don't remember any Blue Man."

"You don't?" laughed Joe. "Hell, he's the weirdest of the lot!"

"Are you sure you didn't count the Man of Many Colors twice?" said Thaddeus sharply.

Joe shrugged. "Take a look for yourself if you don't believe me."

"Tojo," said Thaddeus, "stick your head in there and see if we've got a Blue Man."

I walked over to the first van. I was too small to peek in the window, so I opened the door while Dave stood beside me, brandishing his pistol.

There were six freaks: the Dog-Faced Boy, the India Rubber Man, the Missing Link, the Cyclops, and the two females. I closed the door quickly and walked to the second van. It was dark inside, but I had no trouble seeing the Man of Many Colors: the second the cold air hit him he started changing from bright red to a cool pale blue. There were four others that I recognized, and then I saw a movement just behind the driver's seat. There was something bluish there, making the same grunting and growling noises I had heard behind the locked door of the sideshow. I caught a glimpse of a satanic countenance,

31

much more evil and hideous than that of the Horned Demon, and I slammed the door shut.

"He's there," I said, shuffling hastily back to where Thaddeus stood.

Thaddeus started peeling off 120 bills, while Joe leaned forward and helped him count them.

"I'm still surprised Ahasuerus hasn't made a move yet," said Thaddeus.

"If he does, we'll know what to do with him," Joe assured him. "I wonder how these guys have stayed in business so far. I paid a little visit to their show the other night and told Romany that a couple of the games looked rigged, and you know what he did?"

"What?"

"Closed them up!" laughed Joe.

"He just doesn't understand the role of law enforcement officers in a free-market society," said Thaddeus. He smiled with Joe, but I could tell that he was disturbed, and I knew what he was thinking: what kind of carny manager doesn't know enough to grease a few palms when he hears a pitch like that?

We heard a sudden commotion coming from inside the barn, and all three cops jumped.

"It's probably just a cat killing a field mouse," said Thaddeus. "Still, I suppose we ought to get this show on the road. Tojo, have Jupiter back his bus up to the vans."

I directed Monk as he maneuvered the huge bus into place, and then helped him unlock the various cages. Then, with all three cops standing guard, we began moving the freaks one at a time. The Elephant Woman, her huge watermelonlike head swaying gently, almost lost her balance, and if Monk hadn't caught her she would have fallen, but otherwise we had no trouble with the first van.

The Man of Many Colors was bright green when I opened up the second van. He walked meekly into the bus, followed by three of the others. The Sphinx seemed reluctant to move, but the Blue Man touched him lightly on the shoulder (withers?) and then he quickly leaped from the van into the bus and walked right into the cage Monk was standing next to.

Then came the Blue Man. As he climbed down out of the van I got my first good look at him, and it scared me. He stood almost seven feet tall, and was the skinniest person I had ever seen. His eyes were slanted, more so than any Oriental's, and the irises were orange. He had no nose at all, but there were two large slits where his nostrils should have been. His mouth was small and delicate, and looked like it was incapable of smiling. He was totally bald, and I couldn't see any hair where his eyebrows should have been.

His arms and fingers were jointed in strange places, as if a child had drawn a stick figure in a hurry. He drew himself up to his full height and stared right at me. I backed up a couple of steps, until I was standing between Thaddeus and Joe. He looked at Thaddeus and each policeman in turn, his orange eyes seeming to glow inside his bald, angular head. Then he slowly walked up the stairs to the bus. Even Jupiter, who risked his life daily with his animals, backed off as the Blue Man went into the indicated cage and pulled the door shut behind him.

"All set?" asked Thaddeus, and I could see that he too had been affected by the sight of the Blue Man.

"They're upsetting my cats," said Monk, and indeed the two leopards were hissing and spitting at the Sphinx. The lion was right next to the Blue Man, and he just stood there, nose dripping, eyes averted, trembling with fright.

"They'll be okay," replied Thaddeus quickly. "Follow me to the caravan and then stick the bus somewhere in the middle. If we get stopped for any reason, I don't want anyone peeking in there."

"Maybe you should have gotten the Dancer to ride shotgun," grunted Monk, closing up the bus and climbing into the driver's seat.

"You go with Jupiter, Tojo," said Thaddeus.

"I don't want to," I protested.

"Why not?"

"I don't want to ride with *him*."

He knew what I was talking about. "He's locked up safe and sound in a cage."

"I don't care," I said.

"Well, you little bleeding-heart dwarf, you'd better start caring. About *all* of them."

"What do you mean?"

"As of this moment, you're your brother's keeper." He grinned as I tried to protest. "You're the one who feels so

33

damned sorry for them, aren't you—or did I hear you wrong?"

"The others, yes," I said, skipping verbs in my efforts to get my objection out. "But not him."

"All of them," said Thaddeus. The grin was frozen onto his face, but I could tell he wasn't kidding.

"Please!" I said. "Don't make me do it!"

"I can't make you do a damned thing," he said. "But I can sure as hell make you wish you had. Think about it, Tojo."

I was so upset and scared that I actually started sputtering, but no words came out, and finally I sighed and climbed into the bus next to Monk.

"I wonder if the bossman ain't bit off a little more than he can chew," said Monk, as we fell into place behind Thaddeus' trailer.

As if to lend emphasis to his comment, the lion began squealing in terror as we turned onto the main highway and headed off to join the rest of the show.

5.

You wouldn't think that moving from Vermont to Maine would make that much difference in the weather, but it did. There was snow on the ground, and the wind whipped through the tents so fiercely that even the heaters and blowers we set up didn't really keep us warm. The food stands put away their ice-cream freezers and concentrated on pushing soup and coffee.

Thaddeus had fired the ride men while we were still in Vermont, suggesting that they stick around there and try to latch on with the guy who had bought all the rides. He also got rid of Elmer and the rest of the actors; the only people he kept from the freak show were Merrymax and Little Lulu.

Thaddeus was sure that Ahasuerus would show up, bail Romany out, and take after us with a paid posse of head-breakers. And since we were due to head south after our Vermont tour, he took us up to Maine on the assumption that Ahasuerus would never think of looking to the north with winter coming on.

When we arrived at the first town that would let us set up shop, Thaddeus had some of the men erect tents for the freak show, the girlie show, and the specialty show. Then Diggs set up his games, the food stands were assembled, and we were all ready to open.

That was when the problems started. Jupiter Monk presented the first of them.

"Just what do you plan to do with all those freaks?" he said, walking up to Thaddeus, who was directing the placement of some Midway lights.

"Display 'em," said Thaddeus. "What the hell did you think I was going to do?"

Monk shook his head. "That's not what I meant," he said. "What do you plan to do with them between shows?"

"I suppose we'll keep them in your bus," said Thaddeus. "They're safe there."

"That's what I thought you were going to say," said Monk. He drew a deep breath. "They aren't staying in the bus. You'd better find someplace else for 'em."

"What's the matter?" asked Thaddeus with a smile. "Do they make you nervous?"

"They're human beings, Thaddeus," said Monk. "You can't keep them in cages whenever they're not onstage. At least, you can't do it in *my* bus."

"They're a bunch of goddamned freaks and monsters," said Thaddeus. "What do you want me to do—rent them hotel rooms? Hell, half of them aren't built right to use a toilet even if I gave them one."

"I don't care what you say," said Monk stubbornly. "They've got to go. The only time I keep the cats and the bear in those cages is when we drive, and that's just for their own protection, so I won't have to scrape them off the walls and ceiling if we have an accident. You can't do to human beings what I won't even do to my animals."

"It wouldn't have anything to do with the fact that the Blue Man scares the shit out of your lion, would it?" said Thaddeus.

"That's another reason," said Monk, looking uncomfortable.

"Then move the lion," said Thaddeus. "It's less work."

Monk shook his head. "They go, or I'm taking my bus and leaving." I thought Thaddeus was going to hit him, but Monk just backed up a step and laughed. "You lay a finger on me, bossman, and you're going to wake up with a lion in your trailer. He ain't scared of *you*."

Thaddeus unclenched his fist, shrugged, and walked away. A moment later he told Treetop and Big Alvin to put up another tent and connect it to the one he had earmarked for the freaks.

"Once we move them in there," he told them, "you two guys are riding shotgun on them. If even one of them gets away, I'll see to it that you never work again."

It was an empty threat—Thaddeus had no connections out of the carny business, and not that many in it—but they believed him, and an hour later they had the tent up and were moving the freaks, one at a time, into it.

"My God, they stink!" said Thaddeus, inspecting the premises when the last of them had been moved. "See to it that they all shower before tonight, Tojo. Especially the

36

Elephant Woman and the Lizard." He took a deep breath. "Jesus! I don't know how they can stand themselves!"

"We'll need a portable shower stall," I pointed out.

"We've only got one, and it's for the girls."

"Can't you find another?" I asked.

"You think I'm made of money?" he demanded. "These freaks have already set me back twelve thousand dollars, and I haven't made a penny off them yet. Get some soap and water and sponge 'em down."

"All but *him*."

"*Him* too!" snapped Thaddeus. "If they still stink when you're done, borrow some perfume from Alma or Gloria and spray them with it."

"It's cold in there, Thaddeus," I said.

"It's cold everywhere," he said disgustedly. "That's why we call it winter."

"They could catch pneumonia if I wash them down in here," I said. "Can't we trade heaters with the strip show?"

He shook his head. "They work naked. You want *them* to catch pneumonia?"

"Can't we just borrow it long enough to get the baths done?" I persisted.

He thought about it for a moment, then nodded to Treetop. "Bring it in," he said. "But make sure you take it back as soon as he's done."

Treetop nodded, and rolled in a huge blower unit a couple of minutes later.

And, two minutes after that, Gloria stormed into the tent.

"What's the big idea?" she demanded.

"Thaddeus said we could borrow it for a while," I told her.

"Yeah? Well, you tell that son of a bitch that I'm not working until we get it back. Hell, I've got some goosebumps that are bigger than my nipples!"

I was afraid she was going to back up her statement with a presentation of the evidence, but she just glared at the freaks for a minute and then stalked off in search of Thaddeus. He sent for Treetop a few minutes later, and shortly thereafter we lost our blower.

So I filled up a bucket with warm water and soap, and

37

began sponging off the Human Lizard. I apologized to him as I was working, but he looked neither right nor left, never said a word, never even acknowledged my presence.

I went over to the Elephant Woman next. When she saw me approaching she backed away.

"I'm not going to hurt you," I said gently.

I walked toward her again, and again she moved away from me.

"Don't," said a very hoarse, odd-sounding voice.

I jumped, because I knew the direction it had come from.

"Leave her alone," said the Blue Man, leaning against one of the tent's support posts.

"But—"

"She doesn't like water," he said.

"Boy, I'll tell the world she doesn't!" said Big Alvin, wrinkling his nose. "Pheww!"

"How about the others?" I managed to ask.

"If they want to wash, they will bathe themselves," said the Blue Man.

"Can they?" I asked, my eyes scanning the aggregation of oddities and monsters.

"Yes," said the Blue Man. He paused and looked at me, and suddenly seemed a little less satanic. "They cannot produce food for themselves, however."

It occurred to me that they probably hadn't eaten in more than twenty-four hours. Treetop was just returning from setting the blower back up in the girls' tent, and I sent him over to one of the stands for three dozen hot dogs and a dozen cups of coffee.

"Thank you," said the Blue Man.

"You're welcome," I said.

I tried to send Big Alvin out for cots and chairs, but he refused to leave his post, and even Treetop, who had been willing to spend a couple of minutes picking up the food, was afraid Thaddeus would find out if he left long enough to get what I wanted. So I left the tent by myself, and started rounding up such chairs and bedding as I could find. I'm not very strong, and I had to bring them back one chair and one cot at a time. Then I hunted up a batch of blankets. The whole operation took me almost two hours.

"You're very kind," said the Blue Man when I was finished. "I wish there was some way we could thank you."

He stretched out a grotesquely deformed hand, with fingers jointed in all the wrong places. My first inclination was to draw back, but then I remembered how many people in my life had drawn back from me, so I clenched my teeth together just in case I felt an urge to scream when we made contact, and shook his hand. It felt warm and dry, and very strong.

"What does Flint intend to do with us?" asked the Blue Man after a moment's silence.

"The same thing Mr. Ahasuerus did," I said. "He'll display you."

"For how long?"

"Until you stop making money for him."

"I see," said the Blue Man. I thought he tried to frown, but his skin was stretched so tightly over his lean, angular head that he couldn't really change his expression much. Still, he looked satanic again, and I backed away.

"Have no fear, little one," he said as gently as his fierce voice would permit. "I won't harm you."

I told him that that was very comforting to hear, but that I still had work to do. I moved as far away from him as I could and started setting up the cots. Big Alvin figured it would be okay to help me, as long as he didn't have to leave the tent, and we finished in about ten minutes. Then we opened up the chairs. None of the freaks paid us any attention, and none sat or lay down when we were through.

Jupiter Monk came in a moment later, hauling a bale of hay on his back.

"I don't suppose Thaddeus supplied them with a toilet?" he said.

"No," I answered.

"I figured. Well, this'll be better than nothing." He tossed the hay onto the floor and pulled a wire cutter out of his belt. The Blue Man walked over, curious to see what we were doing, and Monk straightened up. "You keep away from me if you know what's good for you!" he snarled, pointing a scarred and calloused finger at him. The Blue Man backed away. "Just keep clear of me!" continued Monk. "You scared my lion half to death, you damned freak!"

He went back to cutting the wire that held the bale together, then took about a third of the pile and placed it against the far end of the tent. He came back, got the rest of it, and carried it to a spot about five feet away from the first pile. Then he got Treetop to help him and strung some rope around the two piles.

"Okay," he said, brushing himself off. "Hang up a few blankets and they'll have a little privacy—and tell Thaddeus that if he doesn't want his million-dollar show coming down with all kinds of diseases that he'd better pop for a couple of toilets before too much longer."

Then he left, keeping his eyes on the Blue Man—much as he did with Bruno the Bear, which was the most dangerous of his animals.

I turned to watch him go, and when I turned back, I almost bumped into the Blue Man, who had wandered over again.

"When you see him outside the tent, please express our gratitude," he said. "I did not mean to frighten him."

"Not much frightens Jupiter," I said defensively. "He's our animal trainer."

"Thank him for us, little one," said the Blue Man.

"I will," I said. "And my name's Tojo."

"Thank him, Tojo."

"What's your name?" I asked.

"You may call me the Blue Man," he replied, and walked away.

Since Big Alvin and Treetop were on duty, I felt it was all right to leave long enough to have some dinner. I ran into Thaddeus doing the same thing at the food stand.

"I can't understand it," he said as I sat down next to him. "I just called Vermont, and Romany is still in the cooler."

"Jupiter says the freaks should have a toilet," I said.

"As soon as they earn it," replied Thaddeus. "So far all the money has been flowing out. Let's let some flow in."

"Jupiter says if you don't—"

"Enough!" he yelled. "If I want to know what Jupiter Monk says, I'll go talk to him!"

We ate the rest of our meal in silence. When I was about to leave, he placed a heavy hand on my shoulder and held me onto my seat.

"Has the Blue Man tried anything funny?" he said.

"Funny?" I repeated.

"He's the one to watch," said Thaddeus.

"He was very nice to me," I replied.

"So you've decided that being a freak is just a matter of outward appearance," he said with a grin. "How broadminded of you."

"Let me go," I said. "I've got to get back to them."

"Tell 'em they're on in two hours," he shouted after me.

When I returned to the dormitory tent a number of them were clustered around the Man of Many Colors, who had been a dull blue ever since we arrived. He was wrapped in blankets, and Big Alvin was standing near him, looking very disturbed.

"What's going on?" I asked.

"The blue guy—not the mean-looking one, the other one—he threw up a few minutes ago. Greenish stuff, a really bad-smelling mess. Then he started shaking, and they put some blankets around him."

I shouldered my way through to where the Man of Many Colors was sitting on his cot. He was trembling slightly, and his eyes looked a little glassy.

"What's the matter?" I asked. "Will you be all right?"

He didn't say anything, and neither did any of the others.

"Is there anything I can get you?" I said.

He shook his head, but didn't speak.

"I'd better get Thaddeus," I said, turning and starting to leave.

"That won't be necessary," said the Blue Man. "But tell Flint that the Man of Many Colors will not be able to perform tonight."

"What's wrong with him?" I asked.

"A chill."

"Well, tell him to wear something besides a pair of shorts," I said.

"That is what he wears," said the Blue Man. I couldn't tell if it was a question or a statement or an explanation, but whatever it was it sounded final. I shrugged and went off to tell Thaddeus.

I found him standing by a phone booth, the receiver next to his ear. He muttered a couple of sentences, then cursed and slammed it down on the hook.

"Damn!" he said. "Ahasuerus *still* hasn't shown up to bail him out!"

"But I thought you wanted him in jail."

"I wanted *both* of them in jail," said Thaddeus. "For all I know Ahasuerus is ten miles behind us." He looked down at me as if noticing me for the first time. "What the hell do *you* want? I thought I told you to stay with the freaks."

"The Man of Many Colors is sick," I said. "He won't be able to go on tonight."

"Like hell he won't!" snapped Thaddeus.

"He really *is* sick," I said. "I just saw him."

"You let these fuckers start goldbricking on the first day and there's no end to it!" said Thaddeus. "Sick, healthy or dead, he goes on!" He paused to light a cigarette. "You tell them that. You especially tell the Blue Man. And tell them that I'm barking the freak show, just so I can keep an eye on 'em."

"Who's doing the girlie show then?"

"Swede."

Swede was a huge blond guy, almost as tall as Big Alvin, who worked the games for Diggs.

"Does he know how?"

"He'll learn," said Thaddeus. "At least he doesn't trip over his own tongue like some people I know. Now you get your ass over to the tent and tell them that everyone works tonight."

I walked back through the lightly falling snow, teeming with bitterness. Swede was happy working the games and fleecing the marks. He probably even resented being forced to bark the strip show. I'd have given everything I had to change places with him, and Thaddeus knew it. I could never be a barker, we both knew that, but he didn't have to make that remark about tripping over my tongue. I don't know why I stammer. Sometimes I think it's because I was quiet for so long when I was growing up that I've got a lifetime's worth of things to say, and they fight each other in a race to get out. I knew I couldn't get up there and talk to a crowd, but he didn't have to talk to me like that, and he didn't have to give it to the one guy on the grounds who would hate it. It was just unfair.

"You look troubled," said the Blue Man as I stalked into the tent.

"Everyone works tonight," I said, "including him." I gestured to the Man of Many Colors. Then I thought about whose fault it was and whose fault it wasn't, and added, "I'm sorry."

"It's not your fault," said the Blue Man.

"Thaddeus doesn't believe he's sick," I said.

"Would it make a difference if Flint examined him himself?" asked the Blue Man.

"None," I said, and the Blue Man uttered a kind of growling sigh.

"What must be, must be," he said softly. He looked at the Man of Many Colors, then turned back to me. "Where is Mr. Romany?"

"In jail."

"For how long?"

"Probably just a few more hours, unless Mr. Ahasuerus decides not to bail him out."

"And if not?"

"Maybe a week."

"Is he well?"

"Nobody said otherwise," I replied.

It looked like he was going to say something else, but just then Big Alvin came over. "It's getting near show time, Tojo," he said uncomfortably.

"So what?" I said.

"I gotta get over to the girl show," he said. "Gloria'll be on in a few minutes."

"Thaddeus said to stay here," I said.

"If I'm not there, he'll make her work strong," said Big Alvin. "I know he will." He clenched his huge fists until the knuckles turned white. "If he makes her get down on the stage and lets those guys start messing with her . . ." His voice trailed off for a minute. "I've never hurt anyone before, Tojo, but if he makes her do that, I'll do something bad to him. So help me God, I will!"

"It's all right," I said. "Thaddeus is working *this* show."

"Then who's the talker for the meat show?"

"Swede," I said.

"Swede," repeated Big Alvin slowly. He thought about it for a moment. "Swede's okay. He won't make her do anything she doesn't want to do."

43

"I'm sure he won't," I told him gently. "Besides, I don't think we've had time to pay off the cops yet."

"All right," said Big Alvin. "I'll stay here. But if Thaddeus isn't barking for the freaks, I'm leaving."

"I wouldn't stop you if I could," I told him truthfully.

We spent a few more minutes just sitting around, and then Thaddeus, all done up in what he called his Elvis suit—gold lamé from his neck down to his shoes, and twirling a gold cane—walked in.

"Okay, move 'em out," he said.

Big Alvin and Treetop escorted the freaks to the adjoining tent, where each was placed on a separate platform that had been set up. When they were all in place Thaddeus covered the front of each platform with a makeshift curtain made of colorful metallic cloth.

"You stick with the Blue Man," he told me. "If he tries anything funny, give a holler."

Then he shoved me onto the Blue Man's platform and pulled the curtain shut.

The crowd entered a few minutes later. I could hear the drone of Thaddeus' voice as he collected them all outside, taunting and teasing them, but it wasn't until he ushered them into the tent that I could make out the words.

"From far exotic Africa," he thundered, "from the forbidden port of Mozambique, from the pits of Hell itself, comes our first exhibit. Stand back a bit, ma'am. He killed the first two white hunters who tried to capture him, and he went after a customer only last week.

"Now you may be wondering why I let you all in free, why there was no cover charge. That's because Thaddeus Flint doesn't work that way. You, young lady, would you step up next to me, please? Right up here. That's right.

"Now ladies and gentlemen, I'm going to let this young lady right here have a free peek at the Human Lizard. She'll tell you what we've got, she'll tell you if we're trying to pull a fast one here. Then I'm going to ask each of you to hand me a crisp one-dollar bill, and if half of you are willing to pay everyone gets to see him. If not, then the show's over and we'll all go home and watch the late movie. Does that sound fair to you?"

I couldn't tell what he did next, but a moment later I

heard a shrill shriek, and then there was a great bustling noise, as if everyone was pulling out money at once.

"And there he is, ladies and gentlemen," cried Thaddeus. "Half man, half lizard, and all mean. What are you hanging back for, Mac—afraid of snakes? Better not let Blondie know it, or she's going to think you're afraid of a lot of things."

On and on he droned for the better part of five minutes. Then he went through the whole thing again with the Cyclops, this time teasing one man into putting up twenty dollars for the whole crowd. He had a different financial pitch for each exhibit, and it sounded like he'd pocketed about six hundred dollars by the time he'd worked his way through the first nine.

The Man of Many Colors was tenth. I couldn't see him, but I could tell that he wasn't changing colors, because Thaddeus started taunting and insulting him, and finally told the crowd that he was going to refund their money for that particular exhibit, because obviously the man was a shirker with no sense of moral responsibility, and that even though a pale blue man was pretty odd, it wasn't what they had paid to see.

The Blue Man made a funny noise deep within his throat and I looked up at him just in time to see a small tear trickle down his cheek.

"Now this next exhibit I'm gonna let you see for free," continued Thaddeus, as still another mass exclamation arose from the crowd. "But that's for one night only. Starting tomorrow this lovely little lady's going to be working next door in our adult entertainment show. She's gonna shake and spin like you've never seen anyone shake and spin, because she's got *more* to shake and spin than anyone you ever saw. Now even though this delicious accident of Nature is going to make her act fifty percent longer than usual, we're not going to charge you fifty percent more money, no sir . . . You looked shocked, madam . . . no? Then envious . . . certainly not broadminded. Oh, you are? Then I expect to see you and that grinning baldheaded ghoul next to you in the front row of the strip show tomorrow night. Is that a promise?"

"*My fault,*" whispered the Blue Man to himself. "*My fault.*"

Thaddeus went on for a few more minutes about all the

natural wonders that were on display at the strip show, put in a plug for Monk and Dancer, told a couple of stories that looked like they were going to be off-color until he got to the punch lines and made everyone laugh more out of relief than humor, and then ushered them out.

The Blue Man and I waited on the platform, wondering why he had been neglected but not willing to risk Thaddeus' wrath by leaving it. Thaddeus brought seven more groups of people in before the evening was over, though he gave up displaying the Man of Many Colors after two more attempts, and never did he pull the curtain back to reveal the Blue Man.

Then he told Treetop and Big Alvin to take the freaks back and start closing up the place, but to leave a certain platform alone. I assumed that he was pointing to us when he said it.

Sure enough, we remained where we were for the better part of twenty minutes, until the place was empty and only one light remained on. Then Thaddeus walked over and pulled the curtain away. There was a huge grin on his face.

"I can be pretty dense sometimes," he said, standing in front of us with his hands on his hips and a cigarette dangling from his mouth. "It took me until this evening to figure out what was going on." He brought his gaze up to meet the Blue Man's. "Mr. Ahasuerus, I presume?"

The Blue Man stared at him, unmoving and expressionless.

"You're crazy!" I said. "This is the Blue Man. He's one of the freaks."

"This is Mr. Ahasuerus, and I don't think he's a freak at all," said Thaddeus, still grinning from ear to ear.

"What are you talking about?" I demanded. "Just take a look at him!"

"*You* look at him, Tojo," said Thaddeus. "Look at *all* of them. I haven't got it all figured out yet, but I do know this: no human parents ever spawned any freaks like this bunch. Still," he added, flashing an enormous wad of bills that he had obviously taken in during the evening, "I'm not one to look a gift horse in the mouth. It's a pleasure having you aboard, Mr. Ahasuerus."

"The pleasure is not mutual," Mr. Ahasuerus replied coldly.

46

6.

"You can't see it from here," said Mr. Ahasuerus, his orange eyes fixed on some unimaginably distant point a billion billion miles away. "It's a pastoral world of sprawling plains and majestic mountains, a world where the sky is so thick with stars that the nights appear like . . . like your Midway when all the booths are lit up."

It was two in the morning, and the carnival had been closed for more than an hour. Thaddeus had replaced Treetop and Big Alvin with two fresh guards, who had taken up positions at opposite ends of the dormitory tent. Most of the aliens were asleep, although two of them—the Rubber Man and the Human Lizard—were tending to the Man of Many Colors, who was still an unchanging shade of pale blue.

I was sitting with Mr. Ahasuerus, sipping a cup of coffee while he toyed with a bowl of soup. Both of us were wrapped in blankets, which afforded us at least a little warmth against the wind that seemed to cut right through the canvas.

"Are they *all* from your world?" I asked.

"No," he said. "There are thousands upon thousands of populated worlds in the galaxy. They come from some of the others."

"Each of you is from a different world?"

"That is correct."

"Including Mr. Romany?"

"Yes."

"Is this the prelude to an invasion?" I asked, surprised that I could remain so calm while embracing so frightening a thought.

Mr. Ahasuerus laughed softly. It was a hideous sound.

"Have I said something funny?" I asked him.

He shook his head. "I laugh only so I will not cry. Haven't you figured it out yet, little one?"

"I guess not," I admitted. "Why *are* you here?"

"We are sightseers," he said bitterly. "We travel the galaxy, visiting those planets that have not yet joined our community of worlds."

"You're *tourists?*" I repeated unbelievingly.

He nodded again. "We masquerade as a sideshow so as to draw the least possible official attention to ourselves. It allows us to observe a cross-section of the populace without revealing our origins or upsetting their political and religious structure."

"This same group goes all over the galaxy?"

"No. We never accept an applicant who differs too greatly from the dominant life form of the planet that we are to visit. Hence, every member of this particular group breathes oxygen, all but two have mastered at least a rudimentary knowledge of your language, and without exception all can eat the same food you eat with very little damage to their systems. When I realized that no native race had blue skin I decided not to display myself. I also had some trepidations about allowing Amphrawse— the one we billed as the Sphinx—to appear."

"He seemed the oddest," I said. "Except for yourself."

"I know," said Mr. Ahasuerus. "But he had saved his money—or what passes for money on his world—for almost three years in order to visit your planet for two weeks. In his single-minded pursuit of his goal he had broken up his—how may I phrase it?—his family unit, which carries far more serious consequences to him than to a native of Earth. How was I to tell him that he must remain in hiding during our stay here?" He paused for a moment, as if recalling the Sphinx's pleas and appeals. "I am glad that he had nothing to do with our present circumstance. It was a poor decision on my part, for it endangered the others." He sighed. "The mind discerns and decides, and the heart vetoes. It is a very inefficient system."

"It seems to be universal," I said.

"Not entirely," he replied, casting a glance in the direction of Thaddeus' trailer.

"Even him," I said.

"You delude yourself," hissed the Human Lizard, who had been listening to us. (I don't mean that he hissed in a dramatic sense; rather, that his voice was so sibilant that

48

nothing he could ever say would sound like anything *but* a hiss.)

"He treats me decently," I said defensively.

"You have very lax standards of decency," said the Human Lizard.

"What do you know about it?" I said irritably. "Thaddeus gave me a job when everyone else laughed at me. He's the only person who treats me like a human being."

"Is this how human beings treat each other?" replied the Human Lizard. He was incapable of intonation, so I couldn't tell if it was a sincere question or a sarcastic one.

"He's got a lot of people to feed," I said. "He's got a lot on his mind."

"Why do you continue to defend him?" said a voice from behind me. I turned and saw Alma standing just inside the doorway.

"What are you doing here?" I asked her.

"I just heard that we have a new girl in the show," she said with open hostility. "I thought I'd come over and find out about it."

She walked through the tent until she came to the Three-Breasted Woman, who was sitting huddled on a chair with a blanket around her. Alma reached out and pulled the blanket away before the Three-Breasted Woman could shrink back out of reach.

"Goddamnit!" she said. "How the hell are we supposed to compete with *that*? Why don't you stay with the freaks where you belong?"

The Three-Breasted Woman stared up at her in terror, and Mr. Ahasuerus walked over.

"She does not speak English very well," he said gently, interposing himself between the two of them.

"Then how the hell did she convince Thaddeus to let her out of the freak show?" demanded Alma.

"It was not a matter of choice," said Mr. Ahasuerus.

Suddenly Alma's whole attitude changed. "You mean Thaddeus is making her do it?"

Mr. Ahasuerus nodded.

"Does she know what she's getting into?" said Alma.

"None of us do," replied Mr. Ahasuerus.

She turned to me. "And you let him do this, you evil little man!"

"How could I stop him?" I said.

49

"All right, goddamnit!" she snapped. "I'll go talk to him myself!"

She turned on her heel and left.

"Will she succeed?" asked Mr. Ahasuerus softly.

I shrugged. "I don't know."

"What will happen if she doesn't?"

"Let's worry about that when it happens," I said, not wishing to think about it, but thinking about it anyway. Maybe it wouldn't be so bad, even if Thaddeus made her go through with it. After all, she acted like a hootch dancer anyway. Maybe she was a stripper on her home world. Maybe she could even put on a show that would shock Alma.

I asked Mr. Ahasuerus what the Three-Breasted Woman did when she wasn't touring the galaxy.

"She is a . . . I don't know your analog word for it. She participates in her religion."

"Like a nun?" I asked.

"What is a nun?"

I told him, and he replied that that pretty much defined what she was.

"Is she—uh—sacrosanct?" I asked, fumbling for the proper word.

"I don't understand."

"Celibate?"

He didn't know that word either, but when I managed, with much blushing and even worse stammering than usual, to explain it to him, he nodded and said that it was his understanding that all active practitioners of her religion were celibate.

"Oh, brother!" I muttered.

He must have sensed my distress, because he fell silent. After a few more minutes of unsuccessfully trying not to think of what lay in store for a celibate nun in a meat show, I trudged over to the Man of Many Colors, who was lying very still on one of the cots, while the Human Lizard and the India Rubber Man took turns rubbing his wrists vigorously and mopping sweat from his forehead.

"What's the matter with him?" I asked.

"Exposure to the cold," hissed the Human Lizard.

"But the rest of you were exposed to it," I said.

The Human Lizard turned and stared at me with his dead eyes. "In case it has escaped your notice, may I point out that we are not all alike? He comes from a hot arid land, hotter even than my own world. When he is healthy he glows a livid red; when tired, a bright green. He has the capacity to change colors from red to yellow to brown almost at will. But blue is the death color. As it grows paler, he grows weaker; when it vanishes, so too will his life."

"Then shouldn't we move him closer to the heater?" I suggested.

"Would you throw a drowning man into the desert?" replied the Human Lizard. "Or would you remove the water from his lungs? We must make him well, not hot."

"Is there anything I can do to help?" I asked.

He merely stared at me again, and then turned back to the Man of Many Colors.

I walked back to my chair and sat down, feeling absolutely useless. It was not an unfamiliar feeling.

I must have dozed off, because the next thing I knew Alma was standing in front of me, shaking me by the shoulders.

"What is it?" I said, blinking my eyes. "What's happened? Did he die?"

"Who?" she said, confused.

"The Man of Many Colors."

"How the hell would I know?" she said hotly, and I could tell by her face that she was terribly upset about something. "But you can tell the one with the three boobs that she can stay with the freak show."

"I'm very glad to hear that," I said.

"Bully for you."

"Why are you crying, Alma?"

"He had another one of the fucking locals in there with him!" she snapped.

"I'm sorry," I said. I pretended to have more difficulty getting the words out than was true, so I wouldn't have to say anything else, because I couldn't think of anything else to say.

"Doesn't he care about anything, Tojo?" she said, tears streaming down her face. "Doesn't he know what he's driving me to do?"

"I don't understand what you mean," I said.

"I mean that everybody needs a certain amount of human affection," she said, wiping her face with a crumpled

51

piece of Kleenex. "Everybody needs warmth, and comfort, and to know that they're wanted."

"But not everybody can have it," I said softly.

Suddenly she looked down at me as if she had heard me for the first time. "Oh, Tojo, I'm sorry! I didn't mean—" She stopped in midsentence, leaned over, and kissed me on the cheek. "Oh, God!" she muttered, straightening up. "I hope he dies!"

She turned and left again, and this time I knew she wouldn't be back.

I walked over and told Mr. Ahasuerus that the Three-Breasted Woman would be staying with the other aliens.

"Perhaps there is a germ of decency in him after all," said Mr. Ahasuerus.

"Perhaps," I said, though I knew it was far more likely that he had merely agreed to get rid of Alma and avoid a prolonged scene in front of his latest bedmate.

I fell asleep again, and didn't wake up until Gloria and one of the other girls brought in some breakfast—hot dogs and coffee, as usual—and the aliens began waking up.

Then, at about nine o'clock, Jupiter Monk walked in, leading Bruno the Bear by a short chain. Bruno was wearing a muzzle and pulling a huge portable toilet behind him, and Monk guided him to a corner where the straw was stacked. Then he unhooked Bruno's harness, wheeled the toilet around so that the door was facing us, and stood back, hands on hips, to admire his contribution.

"Don't all rush up to thank me at once!" he said in a loud, irritated voice.

"I'm sure everyone is extremely grateful," I said. "On the other hand, I don't think you have to worry about people rushing up to thank you as long as you've got Bruno with you."

"Bruno wouldn't hurt a fly," said Monk, slapping the bear on the head while ducking a vicious swipe of the animal's paw. "People, maybe," he added with a grin.

"I thought we didn't have any toilets," I said, trying to keep Monk between Bruno and myself.

"There weren't any *available*," corrected Monk.

"So how did you get this one?"

"I won it from the Rigger!" laughed Monk. "I just hope he freezes his cock off pissing in the snow!"

"You won it? How?"

"I suckered him," said Monk, looking inordinately pleased with himself.

"No one suckers Diggs."

"Well, he takes a special kind of suckering, that I'll have to admit," said Monk. "He's such a devious bastard that he's always looking for the angle. I gave him a straight bet, and when he couldn't figure out the catch, he finally put up the toilet against two hundred dollars just to find out what the answer was. Don't worry about old Rigger, though; if he doesn't turn into one funny-looking snowman, he'll make a couple of thousand dollars off his learning experience."

"What was the bet?" I asked him.

"I bet him that I could name a Triple Crown race in which half the field went off at odds-on. Well, right off the bat, he said it was Man O' War's Belmont Stakes, because there were only two horses and Man O' War paid something like one cent on the dollar. But I told him no, it wasn't a sucker bet, and that it was a field of six." Monk paused for effect. "Well, this drives him batty, because the way the tote board figures the odds, it's impossible for more than two horses to go off at odds-on, and even then the rest of the field would all be fifty-to-one or more. So he rants and he raves and he refuses to bet, and I leave his trailer, but I know it's going to keep eating away at him until he figures it out. He knows there's an answer, because I'm willing to put up two hundred bucks on the spot, and it's driving him crazy. He even calls a couple of bookies, but they tell him it's impossible, and that drives him even wilder. Finally he can't stand it anymore, so he tells me to come over and pick up the toilet, but he's gotta know the answer."

"*Was* there an answer?"

"Sure," grinned Monk. "Bold Ruler and Gallant Man were both odds-on in the 1957 Belmont Stakes. Field of Six."

"But that's only two," I pointed out.

"Just what the Rigger said. But there was another horse in the field called Bold Nero. By himself he would have been about a trillion-to-one, but he had the same owner as Gallant Man, so they ran as an entry. One owner, one betting interest—so he was odds-on too. If

53

you listen real carefully, you can still hear the Rigger screaming foul."

"Well, we thank you for the toilet," I said.

"You're welcome. It may seem to all assembled here that I'm preoccupied with shit, but actually I'm just working out the foolishness of my youth."

"I don't understand you," I said.

"Go spend a winter capturing Kodiak bears on the Klondike and you'll understand my obsession with the comforts of home," he said with a laugh. "Anyway, I'm glad to have been of help. I've been saving that little bet to pull on Diggs for two years; I guess I found the right time for it."

Bruno started getting restless then, so Monk gave him a couple of smacks on the head and led him out, and Big Alvin, who was back on guard duty, started hauling the straw away.

I checked on the Man of Many Colors. He was still the same pale blue, neither richer nor lighter in color than he had been the night before. The Horned Demon and the Three-Breasted Woman were tending to him now, and after their demeanor convinced me that my help wasn't wanted, I walked over to the table Gloria had set up and had a cup of coffee.

"An interesting beverage," said the India Rubber Man, who was standing nearby, also drinking coffee.

"What do you drink on your world?"

"I couldn't describe it very well," he said. "You have no analog words for it."

"Can you tell me what your world is like?"

"It's a world, like any other."

"I've never been to any other," I said.

"It has people, some good, some bad. We live and die, love and hate, worship and fear. We try to get through each day without causing irreparable harm to those we care for."

"But what of its physical features?" I asked.

"Just props," he said with a shrug that began at his shoulders and wound up in the vicinity of his boneless toes. "I should have thought that you, of all these people, would find physical features unimportant."

"But to see other worlds," I persisted. "It must be—"

"They are simply stages. It is the players who are important."

"Why did you choose to come *here?*"

He shrugged again, in an equally disquieting way. "Because you were here. Because I have never been here. Because I wanted to know what you are like."

"Are we very different from the others you have visited?" I asked.

He shook his head, and for a minute I thought it would twist right off. "No. People are people. They have needs and desires, lusts and fears. I must confess, however, that *you* are a puzzle to me."

"Me?"

"Yes. Why are you content to let him abuse you?"

"Him? You mean Thaddeus?"

"Yes."

"He abuses other people, too. Why single me out?"

"Because they resent him, and you don't."

"Do you like appearing as a freak in a sideshow?" I responded.

"It is an acceptable camouflage."

"But you wouldn't want to do it for your entire life?"

"No," he said firmly.

"Neither would I," I replied. "I have a home here. This is my family. Even the marks treat me as if I belong."

"I understand this," said the Rubber Man. "But why must you stay with Flint? Why not go to another carnival, another sideshow?"

"Because you don't leave your family just because someone else belongs to a happier one," I said. It seemed a lot more convincing when I thought of it than when I finally got the words out. How do you tell a man with no bones who is half a galaxy from home what it means to finally *have* a home?

"The Rubber Man gave me a look that implied that I was even stranger than he had first supposed, and wandered off to join his companions.

A few minutes later Big Alvin and Treetop took them off to their platforms, and as I heard Thaddeus' voice filtering back to the dormitory tent I felt a little of the resentment that the Rubber Man had been unable to perceive. But I felt something else, too: I felt the cord that bound me to Thaddeus Flint and his world—*my* world—

55

with its infinite variety of grotesques. It was a lifeline, it supplied me with comfort and sustenance, and I knew that nothing would ever pry my clutching fingers loose from it.

And then I thought of Thaddeus, driven by whatever personal devils made him the way he was. We are all prisoners of our needs, and since Thaddeus' needs were so much greater than mine or Alma's or Monk's or anyone else's, I couldn't help feeling that he was clutching his end of the cord tighter than any of the rest of us.

7.

Within three days the Man of Many Colors was well enough to be placed on exhibit with the other aliens, although Mr. Ahasuerus told me that his colors were nowhere near as bright as before he'd fallen ill. The Three-Breasted Woman, once she understood what Thaddeus had originally planned for her, became much more subdued in front of the marks, and positively virginal whenever Thaddeus was around. The others went through their paces, some bitterly, some with nothing more than resignation. I think they all looked to Mr. Ahasuerus to pull some rabbit out of the hat and free them, but the blue man seemed to have neither the will nor the ability to act. Besides, he was stranded on an alien planet, and I very much doubt that he could have found his way back to his spaceship without asking the locals for aid—and it has been my experience that people will pay good money to gape at an oddity long before they'll help him for free.

After a couple of days Queenie decided that our "freaks"—no one but Thaddeus and I knew what they really were—needed a cook more than our nude dancers needed a costumer, and she set up a makeshift kitchen in the dormitory tent and went to work preparing their meals, after which the quality of food the aliens ate increased dramatically.

The day after the Man of Many Colors returned to the sideshow was payday, and after the carnival had been closed up and the aliens bedded down, I wandered over to Thaddeus' trailer to pick up my money. When I entered I found him with Jupiter Monk and Billybuck Dancer. They were sitting around talking and drinking beer, and Thaddeus told me to join them.

I could tell that Thaddeus was in a good mood. He had taken in more money during the past four days than he had ever seen before, and he was smiling happily as

Monk related a humorous tale of his first hunting expedition.

"Needed fifteen gibbons for some zoo or another," Monk was saying, "and they placed so damned many restrictions on hunters that I wasn't even allowed to carry a rifle. I mean it. So I finally hunt up a huge family of gibbons, and I start giving orders to my porters and trackers, and they start spouting Marxist philosophy, and finally they go on strike. We negotiate for two days, and then they just up and leave. The only thing they left behind was a truck, a batch of wood cages, and my supply of booze.

"So, given my situation, I figured the only thing I could do was to get the gibbons drunk. I mixed up a huge batch of fruit punch, flavored with about a dozen fifths of vodka, and left it out for 'em. It took 'em a day to walk up and start drinking it, but within a few hours the whole goddamned tribe was so drunk they couldn't see straight. Then it was just a matter of rounding them up and tossing them into the cages."

"They let you do it?" I asked.

"Well, some of them were so drunk they didn't give a damn what the hell I did. The others did put up a fight, but I was sober and they were drunk. I got cut up pretty bad, but within half a day I had my fifteen gibbons. So I deliver them and get an order for ten more, and I go out with an old-time tracker, a guy who ain't heard of Marx or Engels or Patrice Lumumba, and we hunt up some gibbons, and I pull out the medical kit and tell him how to patch me up after I drag them into the cages, and he kind of smiles and says that people have been getting monkeys and apes drunk for centuries, but I was the first guy who would rather wrestle with them than put the drinks inside the cages to begin with! So we did it his way and had our quota inside of an hour."

Thaddeus laughed so hard I thought he was going to spill his beer. The Dancer smiled politely, but as always I had a feeling that his mind was far away and long ago.

"How about you, Dancer?" said Monk. "Ever shoot any animals with those pearl-handled pistols of yours?"

"I don't shoot animals," he said in that gentle Texas drawl of his.

"What's the good of being a marksman if you don't go hunting now and then?" persisted Monk.

"I don't like shooting at things that haven't got a chance to shoot back," said the Dancer.

"Hey, Dancer," said Thaddeus, "is it really true that you outgunned a bandit down in South America?"

The Dancer shrugged noncommittally.

"Well, if it was me, I'd sure as hell brag about it," continued Thaddeus. "If you're the best, you want everyone to know it."

"If you're the best," said the Dancer pleasantly, "you don't much care what anyone else thinks."

"What *do* you care about?" said Thaddeus. "It sure as hell isn't money." He turned to us. "You know that I send his paycheck home to his mama every week?"

He started laughing again, but something about the Dancer's expression made him stop.

"You feed me and house me and pay for my bullets," said the Dancer after a long, uncomfortable pause. "What do I need money for?"

"Everyone needs money," said Thaddeus fervently.

The Dancer shook his head. "Everyone *wants* money. That's not the same thing, Thaddeus. What would you do if you *had* all the money you wanted?"

"Get the hell out of this business," said Thaddeus devoutly.

"No you wouldn't, Thaddeus," said the Dancer.

"Oh?"

"You like fleecing marks, and you love playing God," continued the Dancer. "Money's just a measure of how well you do it."

Thaddeus stared at his glass for a long moment. Then it was his turn to shrug. "Maybe you're right. About staying, that is. Not about the money, though. If nothing else, money buys you a higher class of woman."

"A higher class of woman would dump you quicker than Dancer can draw his gun," laughed Monk. "Not everyone is as understanding as Alma, or as hungry for a spotlight as some of the locals you drag in here, Thaddeus."

Thaddeus uttered a harsh, contemptuous laugh.

"Not all women will put up with being treated like shit," persisted Monk.

Thaddeus stared hotly at Monk and the Dancer, then turned suddenly to me.

"Well?" he demanded.

"Well what?" I said.

"Everyone else is dumping on me. How about you?"

"I don't think you treat women any differently than you treat men," I said cautiously.

"That's my whole point," said Monk with a smile. "Tojo, it's a shame you're such a tongue-tied little bastard. They could use you in the State Department."

"He's my emissary to the freak tent," said Thaddeus.

"Speaking of the freaks, how are they doing?" asked Monk. "I haven't had a chance to drop by for a couple of days."

"All right," I said.

"How about the rainbow man?"

"He's better."

"Hey," said Monk, "that's not a bad name for him."

"The Rainbow Man?" repeated Thaddeus, toying with the suggestion.

"Oh, not for the marks," said Monk hastily. "Whatever you're calling him is good enough for them. But on the assumption that you don't intend to return the freaks to Mr. Ahasuerus"—he paused to see what Thaddeus would say, but Thaddeus just stared at him—"we ought to give them carny names. I mean, who the hell is going to walk up and say, 'How's it going, India Rubber Man?' I think we ought to call the sick one Rainbow."

"Fine by me," said Thaddeus. "And the India Rubber Man?"

"Easy: Stretch," replied Monk.

"Maybe they already have names," I said.

"Maybe we all do," said Monk. "Is your name Tojo?"

"It is now," I said.

"And mine's Jupiter now," said Monk. "So what's wrong with giving names to the freaks?"

"All but the Blue Man," said Thaddeus.

"You know his name?" asked Monk.

"No," said Thaddeus. "I just don't want you talking to him."

Well, they tossed ideas around for half an hour while I listened and Billybuck Dancer stared off into space, and they came up with seven more names. Along with Rainbow and Stretch, the Dog-Faced Boy was Snoopy; the Human Pincushion was Bullseye; the Missing Link was Dapper Dan; the Horned Demon was Scratch (for Old Scratch, I guess; they agreed on it so quickly that I was never quite sure of the source); the Cyclops, with true carny logic, became Four-Eyes; the Human Lizard was Albert the Alligator (Monk was a passionate *Pogo* fan, even though the strip had ceased publication years ago, and he once showed me a scrapbook in which he had pasted a three-year run of daily strips); and the Sphinx was Numa (though Thaddeus thought he looked more like a horse than a lion, and put up quite a fight for calling him Seattle Slew before yielding when Monk started explaining what a Sphinx was supposed to be).

That left the two women.

"You look at the head of the Elephant Woman, and what pops to mind?" said Monk.

"That I'm having a bad dream," replied Thaddeus.

"Well, when I look at her, I think of a watermelon," said Monk.

"Yeah, I can see that," agreed Thaddeus.

"So how about calling her Melon?"

"No good," said Thaddeus, shaking his head. "When I look at the Three-Breasted Woman, all I see is melons."

"You've got a point," said Monk. "Hey, Dancer—what do you think?"

They both turned to the Dancer, but he was staring off at some vision only he could see, oblivious to everything that was being said.

"He's a little worse than usual tonight," remarked Thaddeus.

"Don't knock it," replied Monk. "We all try to shut the carnival out of our minds. He just does it a bit better than most."

"I knew a kid like that when I was growing up in California," said Thaddeus. "Finally one day he just stopped eating and talking and moving. They had to carry him off to the funny farm; I mean, they just lifted him where he stood and hauled him away. I don't think he even knew what was happening to him."

"You grew up in California?" asked Monk, dropping the subject of Dancer's trancelike state.

"Yeah. Can't you tell a beach boy when you see one?"

61

"What did your parents do?"

"They were divorced. My mother was a nurse. I never knew my father well."

"Dead?" asked Monk.

"I suppose so. MIA."

"What does that mean?"

"Vietnam. Missing in action. They never found out what happened to him. He was there when they still called us advisers."

"Tough break," said Monk. "Do they have carnies in California?"

"Not like this one," said Thaddeus.

"Now that we've got those freaks, I don't imagine *any-body* has one like this one."

"That's not what I meant," replied Thaddeus. "They've got games and Ferris wheels, but it's all kind of scrubbed, if you know what I mean. Gotta compete with Disneyland."

"No meat shows?"

"Uh-uh. Strange, isn't it? Seems to me they'd figure out that the only way to compete is to give 'em what they can't get at Disneyland, like meat shows and freak shows."

"Maybe we ought to head off for California," suggested Monk.

"Too many cops to pay off," said Thaddeus.

"You've got the freaks now," Monk pointed out. "You could get rid of the girls and go legit."

For just a minute a strange look came over Thaddeus' face, as if he was actually considering it. Then the wistfulness vanished.

"Too many problems," he said at last, and I knew he was thinking of Mr. Ahasuerus. "Besides, the girls bring in more money than you and the Dancer do."

"Well, I'm a little past my prime, but I'd venture to say that if Billybuck let the ladies do to him what the men do to the strippers, he'd match them dollar for dollar."

I shot a quick glance at the Dancer, but he was still oblivious to what was being said.

"He'd probably shoot them all," replied Thaddeus with a dry chuckle. "I wonder how the hell he ever got to be so good with a gun?"

"Why not ask him?" suggested Monk.

"Take a look at him," said Thaddeus. "He's off in Dodge City or Tombstone, protecting proper young ladies and their maiden aunts from the Clanton Brothers."

I wouldn't have bet against it. He had that faraway look on his face, the look of a dreamer at work. I guess this business makes dreamers of us all; the Dancer just gives in to it more readily. But Monk dreams of working in the center ring of a real circus, Alma dreams of respectability, Thaddeus dreams of God knows what. And me—I dream of being six feet tall and having perfect diction. The only thing we have in common is that none of us is ever going to realize those dreams.

"Well," said Monk, taking a final swallow and setting his empty glass down on a table, "I've got to go and clean up after my animals."

"Take Wild Bill Hickok with you," said Thaddeus.

Monk poked the Dancer on the shoulder, and he rose with the same animal grace as one of the leopards.

"Thank you for the beer, Thaddeus," he said, touching his fingers to his Stetson and walking out the door. Monk just chuckled, shook his head, and followed him.

"How about you?" Thaddeus asked me. "Are all *your* animals clean?"

"They're not animals," I said.

"How about the Elephant Woman? Have you found a way to bathe her?"

"Yes. I had Gloria stop at a pet store when she went into town to do some shopping. She bought a kind of dry shampoo they use on show dogs."

"Good," said Thaddeus.

"I'm surprised that you give a damn," I said.

He looked uncomfortable. "I've got to protect my investment," he said hastily.

I didn't know what to say next, but something about his attitude led me to believe that he wanted to talk further, and I knew that if he did he certainly wouldn't think twice about physically restraining me if I tried to leave.

"You never mentioned that you were from California," I said, trying to make conversation.

"Is it that hard to believe?"

"No. It's just that you never speak about your past."

"It's not important," he said. "Today and tomorrow are

63

all that count. You start thinking about yesterday and you're likely to wind up like the Dancer."

"Was it nice out there?"

"It was warmer," he said with a smile. "And the girls—well, the song is right. There really *is* something different about California girls. I used to lay on the beach and watch them go bouncing by, spilling out of their bikinis. It was a nice way to grow up. I'll tell you something, Tojo: California girls never say No. Never once."

He leaned back, his eyes half closed, a smile on his face as if he were reliving his days in the sun.

Suddenly he sat up. "I'll tell you something else, too: you'd never catch one of them working in a meat show. They've got too much class."

"You shouldn't talk about the strip show like that," I said. "They're decent people, Alma and the others—and they pay your bills."

"You look at it all wrong, Tojo," he said. "Someday it'll drive you crazy."

"What do you mean?"

"Decent people don't do what *they* do for a living," he said slowly, taking a long swallow from the bottle. "You've heard them talk about it. It's like they're spectators and the audience is providing the show. It's the only way they can live without going nuts—they've got to shut off all their emotions. You've got to do the same thing. You start thinking of them as decent people and suddenly you can't let them go on, and then where would we all be?"

Suddenly he looked embarrassed, as if he said more than he meant to.

"Talk about something else, you goddamned dwarf," he said irritably. "And stop staring at me like that."

"What do you want me to talk about, Thaddeus?" I asked him.

"I don't know. How are the freaks doing?"

"They're unhappy. And they're not freaks—they're aliens."

"Whatever," he muttered. He finished his beer and opened another. "Why the hell do you suppose they came here? I mean, wherever they lived, it couldn't be *this* grubby."

"Curiosity," I said.

64

"Just like the girls," he said. "They let the audience put on a show for them."

A frown crossed his face, and I could tell that he had just drawn the parallel one step further, and realized that he was forcing himself to view them as he viewed the strippers.

"You know, you're pretty lousy company tonight," he said.

"I'm sorry."

He rose unsteadily to his feet.

"I think I'll hunt up Alma and bring her back here," he announced.

"I don't think it would be a good idea," I said.

"Why the hell not?"

"She's mad at you."

"Big deal," he said. "She's always mad at me."

"This time is different."

"Every time is different," he said, lurching toward the door.

I walked over and stood in front of the door.

"Don't, Thaddeus," I said.

"You're hiding something, you little wart," he said. "What is it?"

"Nothing."

"Out with it!" he yelled.

"She's spending the night in Queenie's trailer," I said softly.

"Are you trying to tell me she's a fluff butch?" he demanded with a harsh, unbelieving laugh. "Because I happen to be in a position to know that she's not."

"No," I said. "I'm trying to tell you that she's hurt and lonely, and that she's found a way to feel less hurt and less lonely."

He frowned again, and for a minute I thought he was going to hit me. Then he uttered a deep sigh and walked back to his chair.

"You're really not kidding," he said quietly, after staring out the window for well over a minute.

"No, Thaddeus."

"She hates me that much?"

"It's not a matter of love or hate," I said. "It's a matter of need."

"But *Queenie,* for Christ's sake?"

"Queenie cares."

"Queenie can *afford* to care," he said bitterly.

We sat in total silence while he drank two more beers and started in on a bottle of rye. Then, almost without warning, he passed out.

I knew I wasn't strong enough to carry or even drag him to the bedroom, so I covered him with a blanket, turned out the lights, and returned to the dormitory tent, wondering if he was dreaming about Alma or about golden-skinned California girls with tasteful bikinis and gently swelling breasts and ready blushes, who would live and die without knowing that anyone like Alma even existed.

8.

The Cyclops—I think I'd better start calling him Four-Eyes, like everyone else does—was very sick the next morning.

Mr. Ahasuerus shook me awake just before dawn, apologized for disturbing me, and led me over to where Four-Eyes was sitting. I didn't have to be an alien physiologist to know he was in a bad way. He was trembling violently, his pupil was completely dilated, his tongue was coated, sweat was pouring down his body, and he felt hot to the touch.

"How long has he been like this?" I asked.

"About two hours," said Mr. Ahasuerus. "I hadn't wanted to bother you, but it's too serious to leave him unattended."

"What's the matter with him?"

"I think his system finally rebelled against the food he's been eating," replied Mr. Ahasuerus. "When I told you that we could tolerate a certain amount of your native food, I should have pointed out that our entire stay on your planet was to be no more than fourteen days."

"How long have you been here?" I asked.

"Only eleven," he replied, "but it obviously affects some of us more rapidly than others."

I took another look at Four-Eyes.

"I'd better get Thaddeus," I said, and headed off to his trailer.

He was lying exactly as I had left him, sprawled on a small couch with his arms and legs dangling over the sides, and covered with a faded purple blanket. I woke him up and told him that he'd better get over to the dormitory tent right away.

I've seen him spend an hour crawling out of bed when he's got a hangover, and I've seen him stay asleep with Monk's lion roaring right outside the window—but mention that the carnival's got a problem and he's up and alert in ten seconds. Since he was already dressed, all he did was splash some cold water on his face and, without even bothering to put on a jacket, he ran across the snow-covered Midway to the aliens' tent without saying a word. I guess he must have thought Mr. Ahasuerus was leading a revolt or something like that, because he looked surprised to see the total lack of commotion when he arrived.

"What's up?" he asked me.

"Four-Eyes," I said. "He's very sick."

"Who the hell is that?"

"The Cyclops. You named him last night."

"Oh, yeah. Right." He walked over to Four-Eyes, then turned to Mr. Ahasuerus.

"Just how bad is he?" he demanded.

"I don't know," answered Mr. Ahasuerus.

"Why the hell not?" snapped Thaddeus. "You're the goddamned tour guide, aren't you?"

"I am not a doctor," said Mr. Ahasuerus. "And he needs one."

"Well, we don't happen to have any doctors who specialize in one-eyed men from Mars," said Thaddeus. He picked up Four-Eyes' hand in his own and took his pulse. "What's the normal rate for this guy?"

"I have no idea," replied the blue man.

"Is there anything about him that you *do* know?" asked Thaddeus contemptuously.

"I think the food has made him sick."

"I notice that it didn't make anyone else sick," said Thaddeus, "or do you all intend to start foaming at the mouth and collapsing?"

"We are all different," said Mr. Ahasuerus. "This is an alien environment. It affects us in different ways."

Thaddeus dropped Four-Eyes' hand and frowned. "Find out from him what he needs and we'll try to supply it."

"He needs freedom," hissed Albert the Alligator.

"You can't eat freedom," said Thaddeus coldly. He turned to Mr. Ahasuerus. "Find out what it is: potassium, iodine, whipped cream, whatever."

"What if he can't reply?" asked Mr. Ahasuerus.

"Then you'll have to figure out who's guiltier—you or me," said Thaddeus.

He turned and started to leave the tent. I shuffled after him and caught up with him at the doorway.

"Thaddeus, I think he's dying," I said.

"Horseshit," said Thaddeus. "He's got a bellyache."

"But—"

"Look," he said, "if our food could kill him instantly, he'd be dead by now. If it kills him slowly, then he's committed suicide and there's nothing we can do to stop it. And if he was suicidal, he'd have tried to kill himself before now, so what he's got is a pain in the gut. It's probably like eating rich food: one meal is okay, three are okay, and twenty in a row will have you wishing you were dead. Find out what he needs and give it to him—and for Christ's sake, don't let him go back to eating Queenie's food once he's recovered."

"I hope you're right," I said.

"I am," he replied confidently. "And you tell that son of a bitch that I want him back to work tomorrow night at the latest."

It turned out that Four-Eyes needed enormous supplements of iron and sodium. Once Mr. Ahasuerus relayed that information to me I had Gloria buy a batch of each, and within a few hours he was showing a noticeable improvement.

Everything went along smoothly for two more days. Then we experienced the first blizzard of the season. The winds whipped across the landscape at fifty miles an hour, snow piled up everywhere, and we had to shut down just before twilight.

Sometime during the night one of the power lines was knocked down. The county repairmen had it fixed in a couple of hours, but by then Rainbow was pale blue again.

"What the hell did you let him come along for?" Thaddeus demanded of Mr. Ahasuerus after examining the Man of Many Colors. "If he's got any survival traits I sure as hell haven't seen them."

"He would have been all right under normal circumstances," said Mr. Ahasuerus softly.

Thaddeus glared at him. "It could have snowed a week ago," he said.

"But it didn't," replied Mr. Ahasuerus.

Thaddeus turned to me. "Go over to the girls' trailers

and see if any of them have an electric blanket. If not, get a couple of hot-water bottles."

"Thank you," mumbled Rainbow.

"I don't need any thanks for protecting my investment," snapped Thaddeus. He looked around the tent. "Rainbow stays here. Everyone else works. We start at noon."

He walked out without another word.

I managed to borrow an electric blanket from Gloria, and when I returned I plugged it in and showed Rainbow how to use the controls. It was about ten-thirty, and I decided to have some breakfast before the show began.

"I don't understand him," said Scratch, walking over and sitting next to me while I ate some of Queenie's scrambled eggs and bacon.

I fought the urge to edge away from him. During the past week I had made an effort to get to know most of the aliens, but Scratch scared me. Not the way Mr. Ahasuerus had at first, but in a deeper, more mystical way. He was probably a very decent person, and someone had told me that he was a mathematician and poet on his home world, but with his reddish color and the two huge horns growing out of his forehead he seemed diabolical in appearance. Thaddeus had dressed him in red satin, with a black cape, and he looked as if he belonged on the throne of Hell.

"You mean Thaddeus?" I asked, leaning back just a little.

"Yes," said Scratch. "You are a decent man, and you do not hate him, so doubtless he has certain admirable qualities."

I would have been hard-pressed to tell him what they were, so I simply stared at him and waited for him to speak again.

"Yet I find him a mass of contradictions," continued the satanic alien. "He treats our illnesses, yet he won't set us free. He lets his mate perform what in your society are acts of degradation, but he allows her to convince him that the Three-Breasted Woman should not have to undergo such an experience. He treats us like animals, yet yesterday he threatened a customer with physical violence for making a remark far less insulting than those he himself makes all the time. Why?"

I shrugged. "I don't know. Life isn't as simple as I

once thought it was. And, just for the record, Alma isn't his mate."

"But I understood him to say . . ."

"He doesn't always tell the truth," I said.

"Will he ever release us?" asked Scratch.

"I don't know," I told him truthfully.

"Sooner or later we will start dying," he said without emotion. "The food, the air, the temperature, the gravity, even the stress, will do us in. He will cause the death of twelve intelligent entities. Doesn't this trouble him?"

I didn't know how to answer him, so I didn't say anything.

"No, I suppose it doesn't," he continued. He uttered what I took to be an oath. "I ache for my mate and my children. I have my work to return to. What am I to do?"

"I'm surprised you haven't tried to escape," I remarked as casually as I could.

"To what purpose?" he said. "Oh, we have the ability to leave here, even if Flint tried to stop us. But where would we go? What would we do? We could never find our shuttlecraft, and before long our presence would be made manifest to your race."

"Would that be so terrible?" I asked.

"I personally cannot see why it would, but I am told that those few worlds that have been made aware of us have changed radically and unnaturally because of that knowledge. Our most sacred pledge before embarking upon this endeavor was to maintain secrecy at all costs."

Suddenly he didn't seem quite so satanic.

"You're caught between the devil and the deep blue sea," I said.

He didn't understand that, of course, so I had to explain just what the devil was. He was quite amused.

"We have three devils in our religion," he said with a smile. "One of them looks exactly like Monk, and another could be a cousin of Alma's."

"Then I hope you understand why I'm a little nervous in your presence," I said.

"You must not have been watching me very closely when Monk loaded us into his cages," said Scratch. "I was trembling so much from fright that I thought I would faint."

"Three devils," I said. "That's a lot of bogeymen to be afraid of."

"And none of them looks like Flint," he said, staring at the doorway. Then he added in a faraway voice: "Isn't that curious?"

He sat in silence for another moment or two, then wandered off. I checked on Rainbow, who seemed to be in serious discomfort, but there was nothing I could do for him, so finally I went back to the makeshift kitchen and asked Queenie for a cup of coffee.

"Ah, the henchman returns," she said contemptuously.

"I'm not his henchman, Queenie," I said.

"You like 'lackey' better?" she asked.

"I prefer Tojo," I said. "It's my name."

"Did he give it to you?"

"What if he did?"

"He's pretty good at making up names," said Queenie. "He tells a girl who doesn't know any better that he loves her, and then he names her Honeysuckle Rose and makes her go out on a stage and do God knows what with a bunch of sick, retarded hicks!"

"I don't know what you want me to say."

"I want you to say that he's a vicious bastard who ought to have his balls cut off!" she snapped. "Just once, I want you to stand up to him!"

"*You* still work for him," I noted softly.

"Only because Alma's still here," she said. "He's got her mind so messed up that she doesn't know whether she's coming or going. I'll tell you this, though: he's never going to lay a finger on my Alma again, or I'll kill him!"

"Is she *your* Alma now?" I asked.

"She is."

"And has she agreed?"

"She hasn't disagreed." She jutted her chin out. "You got any objections?"

"Not if she's happy," I said.

"I'll make her happier than he would, that's for sure," said Queenie.

"Is she going to keep working in the show?"

"She doesn't care who does what to her," said Queenie, and for a minute I thought she was going to cry. Then her face hardened again. "That's what Thaddeus has done to her. Once she cares again, she'll quit."

"I hope so," I said.

"I know you do," she replied gently. "I'm sorry, Tojo. Sometimes I can't help getting you mixed up with him. God, do you know what it's like lying in bed with her and seeing her looking out the window at his trailer with tears trickling down her face?"

"I know what her face looks like with tears on it," I said.

"It's not the same thing."

"No, I guess not," I answered softly. I thanked her for my coffee and spent the next hour sitting next to Rainbow, looking for a change in his color. There wasn't any, but he did seem a little more comfortable. Then, at noon, I escorted the other aliens to the sideshow tent.

Thaddeus showed up ten minutes late and looking very agitated. His patter was off, and he almost got into a fight with a customer. Finally, just before three o'clock, he told Swede, who was selling tickets, to close up the box office, and after he rushed the last batch of customers through he had me take the aliens back to the dormitory tent.

He entered a minute later, practically snorting fire from his nostrils, and told the guards to wait outside. Then he lined the aliens up and stood in front of them, an ominous smile on his face.

"I just got a phone call from Vermont," he said, looking from one alien to the next. "They released Romany early this morning." He paused for a few seconds, then continued. "He told them he was coming to Maine to look for us."

None of the aliens made any comment, or even moved.

"So I got to thinking about it," said Thaddeus. "How the hell could he know to look for us in Maine, when all logic says we'd be moving south, and when even I myself didn't know we were going to Maine until after he'd been arrested? *I* didn't tell the cops we were going to Maine, and I'm sure none of you told them. So how did he know?"

Silence.

"He knew," said Thaddeus triumphantly, "because one of you goddamned freaks is a telepath! You told him where we are and you're guiding him every step of the way!"

He folded his arms across his chest and glared at them.

"All right," he said. "Who is it?"

Nobody moved.

"Someone is in for a lot of trouble," he said. "What happens to him is going to happen whether it happens to everyone else or not."

"We have been kidnapped and mistreated," said Mr. Ahasuerus at last. "You have deprived us of our physical and spiritual needs. What possible threat can you make at this point?"

"You're still alive," said Thaddeus grimly. "That is not necessarily a permanent condition."

"You won't kill us," said Mr. Ahasuerus with a wry smile. "What would become of your profit?"

"You think about whether I'll make appreciably less profit with six freaks than twelve, and let me know when you come up with an answer," said Thaddeus.

"And *you* think about how you will display us if, for example, we were to go on a hunger strike," said Mr. Ahasuerus.

"Semantics," said Thaddeus.

"I don't understand."

"Whether you go on a hunger strike or I put you on a starvation diet, the result is going to be the same: you ain't gonna have one hell of a lot to eat."

"What must be, must be," said the blue man.

"You think about it real carefully," said Thaddeus. "Just how long do you think the rainbow man can go without food in his current condition? How long can the Cyclops make it without his pills? I want to know today!"

He turned to me. "You come with me!" he snapped. Then he walked out of the tent and headed over to his trailer. I couldn't see that any purpose would be served by defying him, so I paused for just a few seconds and fell into step behind him.

I expected to see him start ranting and raving and throwing things against the walls, but instead he sat on his couch, a self-satisfied smile on his face.

"I guess *that* put the fear of God into 'em!" he chuckled, lighting up a cigarette.

"Didn't you mean it?" I asked.

"Of course not! Who the hell is going to shell out money to see a bunch of dying aliens?"

"Then why did you say it?"

"You got to show 'em who's boss, Tojo," he said.

"Besides, I didn't want them to think I was so goddamned dumb that I didn't know what was going on."

"But when they find out you're not going to do anything—"

"My God, you're as dumb as they are!" he said irritably. "Do you really think I'd grandstand like that if I couldn't follow it up?"

"I don't understand what you mean," I said.

"I told them I wanted the name of the telepath," he said with a grin. "They're going to give it to me."

"They'll never tell you," I said.

"I already know," he said with a laugh. "It's gotta be the Pincushion."

"Bullseye?" I said. "What makes you so sure?"

"Because he's the only one who doesn't talk. How the hell else can he communicate?"

"Then why didn't you accuse him?"

"Divide and conquer," Thaddeus replied. "I'm going to grill each one privately. When I'm done I'll announce that one of them told me."

"But why?"

"Everyone's got a pent-up supply of rage and suspicion," he said. "Why the hell should it all be directed at an honest businessman like me who's just doing his job? A little dissension, a little distrust, a little skepticism about their comrades-in-arms ought to make everything go a little smoother. Who the hell is going to plan a revolution when they've got an informer in the ranks?"

Deep down inside of me I probably knew it all the time, but it was at that instant that I realized beyond any shadow of a doubt that Mr. Ahasuerus and the others had more than met their match.

9.

Thaddeus interviewed the aliens one by one, announced that one of them had told him who the telepath was, and settled back to enjoy the show. They didn't say much, but I could tell that there was a new level of tension in the dormitory tent. I also had a feeling that Mr. Ahasuerus knew exactly what was going on, but, for whatever reason, he made no attempt to offer his associates the true scenario.

Rainbow didn't get any worse, but he didn't get any better either, and by the time Four-Eyes was totally recovered another of the aliens was sick. This time it was Pumpkin, which was the name Monk finally came up with for the Elephant Woman. (I approved of it: it was feminine, and at the same time it described her head as perhaps no other word could do.) It turned out that she had developed a severe skin rash in reaction to the dry shampoo we were using on her, but her skin was so oddly textured and miscolored that she was sick for two days before we could pinpoint the problem.

Thaddeus' first inclination was to wash her down and cover her rash with some kind of salve, but Mr. Ahasuerus assured us that she would react far more violently to water than to the dog shampoo.

"Well, what the hell can we treat her with, then?" demanded Thaddeus.

"Time," replied the blue man. "I think that any foreign substance—and you must understand that *all* of your substances are foreign to her—will merely exacerbate the problem."

I don't think that Thaddeus knew what "exacerbate" meant, but he gave an affirmative grunt and told Pumpkin to stay in the tent until she was better.

Since Rainbow was still under the weather, and Thaddeus never allowed Mr. Ahasuerus to be placed on exhibit, Pumpkin's illness left only nine aliens for the public to see. Business fell off a bit. I attributed it to the increasingly poor weather, and the fact that we'd already been in town for more than a week, but Thaddeus was convinced that the absence of two of the advertised freaks had led some of the people to conclude that they were frauds which had been exposed. It became imperative in his mind to get them back on display, and he spent a lot of time in the dormitory tent supervising their treatment.

Pumpkin wouldn't let him touch her, and even drew back when he merely walked by her, but Rainbow didn't much give a damn who did what to him as long as it made him feel a little warmer, and one evening I walked in to find Thaddeus, his shirt and jacket piled on the floor, sweat pouring off his body, giving the Man of Many Colors a vigorous rubdown. As he did so Rainbow's hue would intensify; when he stopped to rest, the color would become pale again. It was like a war of attrition, which Rainbow finally won since Thaddeus, strong and vigorous as he was, couldn't keep rubbing life and color into Rainbow's limbs and body all night.

"How do you feel now?" he asked, panting, when he had finally given up the battle.

"Better, thank you," said Rainbow, though his color belied his words.

"Just how the hell hot does it get where you live?" asked Thaddeus, grabbing a towel and wiping himself off.

"That's somewhat relative," said Rainbow weakly. "I don't find it hot at all, but it would probably kill you."

"Why did you come *here*, of all places?" continued Thaddeus.

"To see it," said Rainbow.

"Now that you've seen it, was it worth the trip?"

"No," said Rainbow. "No, it was not." He looked up at Thaddeus. "Will you ever let us go?"

"Let's let that remain one of life's little mysteries," said Thaddeus.

He put on his shirt and walked over to me.

"If you're not doing anything later, give him another rubdown," he said.

"It didn't do much good," I replied. "Look at him."

"There's an old story about a spider that kept trying to jump across a gap or climb out of a pit or something," said Thaddeus. "I don't remember exactly how it went, but the gist of it is that if you don't keep trying to get Rainbow back in the show I'm going to kick your ass all over the Midway."

"All right, Thaddeus," I said. "I'll do it."

"I knew I could appeal to your sense of Christian charity," he laughed, and left the tent.

I gave Rainbow another rubdown that night, and again the next morning, and strangely enough his color was a little better after each session.

As the crowds continued to diminish, Thaddeus decided that it was finally time to move on. He felt we had to go at least one hundred miles away, since Maine is so sparsely populated that most of our customers drove more than an hour to get to us. He called the weather service, concluded that it was too cold to continue moving to the north, and decided to head back into Vermont. He never mentioned it, but I'm sure the thought of Mr. Romany searching for us in Maine had something to do with his decision. Obviously Bullseye didn't know exactly where we were, and didn't telegraph the kind of mental signal that Mr. Romany could home in on, or else he would have found us already. I guess "Maine countryside" wasn't enough for him to go on.

We went back to Vermont and set up shop in one of the rural areas after Diggs got us the proper permits. Thaddeus told the aliens we were still in Maine, and then he let Bullseye "overhear" him saying that we were really in New Hampshire and that Mr. Romany would never be able to find us now.

The dormitory tent was getting a grubby, too-well-worn appearance. None of the furniture was really made for the aliens, and it started breaking. Most of them were starting to experience mild digestive problems from the food, too, and we found that winter had followed us to northern Vermont. The wind still cut to the bone, despite the heaters and blowers, and although Pumpkin finally started showing some improvement, Rainbow remained a ghastly shade of pale blue.

The second day in our new location Dapper Dan, the Missing Link, stopped eating altogether. He sat motionless on the edge of his cot, his elbows supported on his knees, his face in his hands, and refused to move. There didn't seem to be anything physiologically wrong with him—at least, there was nothing *we* could spot—and finally Thaddeus decided that he was healthy enough to work. He paid no attention to Thaddeus' order to get up and move over to the sideshow tent, and Big Alvin had to half-drag and half-carry him there.

After the first show Thaddeus had Alvin bring him back to the dormitory tent, where he lay motionless on his cot. Thaddeus kept barking for the show until the crowds diminished in the late afternoon, then stalked into the tent and over to where Dapper Dan lay.

"All right!" he snapped. "Out with it! What the hell are you trying to pull?"

Dapper Dan made no answer.

"There's not a goddamned thing wrong with you!" continued Thaddeus. He reached down and grabbed Dapper Dan by the shoulders, shaking him vigorously. "Admit it, you fucking ape! You're as healthy as I am!"

Dapper Dan made no effort to free himself, but merely met Thaddeus' enraged gaze with an expression that, on his particular face, could have been anything from resignation to boredom.

"Now you listen to me!" Thaddeus bellowed at the top of his lungs, and all the aliens turned to him. "I let Rainbow and Pumpkin stay in here when they're sick, and suddenly the monkey man's trying to pull a fast one! That's what I get for being such a considerate guy. If you goddamned freaks think you can get away with this kind of shit, you've got another think coming! Either Dapper Dan works tomorrow, or he can sit and sulk in the tent and Rainbow and Pumpkin will go on in his place."

"You'll kill them," said Mr. Ahasuerus.

"Not *me*, friend!" snapped Thaddeus. "If Rainbow goes out and turns into a blue popsicle, you'll know who to blame. He's lying right there on his cot. You hear me, apeman? I'll feed you and house you and medicate you when you need it, but you're going to work just as hard as I do, or you're going to wish you had. There's no third way!"

He stalked back out of the tent in the direction of his trailer, and Mr. Ahasuerus walked over to Dapper Dan while the other aliens studiously turned their attention elsewhere.

"What is the matter?" asked the blue man gently.

79

"I cannot tolerate the situation any longer," said the Missing Link. "Let him kill me if he wants. I look into the heavens, and I cannot even find my home star. I will never see my family again." He paused, and turned his gaze directly to Mr. Ahasuerus. "I will not spend the rest of my life as a caged animal, depending on the whim of a madman for such minimal comfort as he chooses to give me."

"There is nothing we can do," said Mr. Ahasuerus.

"We can escape!" said Dapper Dan passionately. "We can kill this evil man and leave!"

Mr. Ahasuerus shook his head sadly. "No, we can't."

"But *why?*" pleaded Dapper Dan, tears filling his eyes. "Why must I die without the sacraments of my religion? Why must I die on this piece of filth spinning around a star that I cannot even find on the charts of my world? Why must my soul be doomed to an eternity of aimless wandering in the void, an unthinkable distance from others of its kind?"

"We made a pledge to keep our existence a secret," said Mr. Ahasuerus.

"*You* made a pledge!" said Dapper Dan.

"So did you," Mr. Ahasuerus pointed out.

"I made a pledge to honor my God on my home world," said Dapper Dan. "I made a pledge to live out my days with the ones I love. Why should this pledge take precedence? It was made to a soulless company that had no idea of the consequences of our journey here."

Mr. Ahasuerus sighed, a terrible sound but somehow touching. "I can't stop you," he said at last. "You are a thinking being possessed of free will, and I have no more right to direct your life than Flint does. But I won't help you, and neither will any of the others. Our word must be our bond, regardless of how you yourself view it." He turned to me. "Tojo, if he were to escape, how far would he get?"

"Not very," I said. "Some of you might, if they didn't shoot you out of fear, but not Dapper Dan. He, more than any of you, resembles a wild animal of Earth. I think the first farmer who saw him would shoot him down. And the first person without a gun who saw him would call the police, and *they* would kill him."

"And even if you avoided them," said Mr. Ahasuerus

gently, "where would you go? How can an alien in a hostile world survive? You don't even know where you are, so how could you find our shuttlecraft?"

"Then it's hopeless, and I shall die here, and my soul will wander aimlessly forever," said Dapper Dan. He lay back down on his cot in an odd and seemingly uncomfortable position which I somehow knew to be his race's equivalent of the fetal position.

"I ask you to consider your fellow beings," said Mr. Ahasuerus. "If you do not go into the sideshow tent tomorrow, one of them will surely die, and the other will at the very least become sicker."

Dapper Dan lay perfectly still. He said nothing, and gave no indication that he had even heard the Blue Man.

Mr. Ahasuerus turned to me. "The truth, Tojo: will Flint do what he said?"

"I don't know," I replied truthfully. "I doubt it. He has no reason to see Rainbow die, and he has a very good financial reason to keep him alive. But if he feels that backing down would weaken his authority . . ." I let my voice trail off—it wasn't hard to do; it trails off all the time—and then looked up at him. "I really don't know."

"I know that he's a greedy man," said Mr. Ahasuerus. "I know that he's selfish and inconsiderate."

"He's not what they call other-directed, that's for sure," I put in.

"But I had not truly conceived of him as a totally evil man, a man who would willingly take a life merely to prove a point."

"I hope you're right," I said. "But just to be on the safe side, maybe you'd better try to convince Dapper Dan to go to work tomorrow."

"I can't force him to do what he doesn't want to do," said Mr. Ahasuerus. "Flint is a shrewd man, and a masterful manipulator, but the fact of the matter is that if the Man of Many Colors dies, it will be Flint and Flint alone who bears the responsibility for it."

"He'll be just as dead either way," I said. "I think you should talk to Dapper Dan."

The blue man uttered a dry chuckle; it sounded like a frog being choked. "He has even made a pragmatist out of *you*, hasn't he?"

"I guess he has," I replied.

Mr. Ahasuerus started walking to the other side of the tent. "Let's let him think," he said softly. "I'll speak to him later."

I had about half an hour to kill before the next show, so I took the opportunity to make a brief tour of the carnival, which I hadn't done in days. I saw Monk leading Bruno the Bear back to his bus, so I knew Billybuck Dancer would be performing in the specialty tent and I went inside to take a look.

He had an assistant—one of the strippers, dressed up in a metallic cowgirl suit—and she was holding four picture cards up where the audience could see them. Then she asked the Dancer if he was ready. He nodded his head slightly—the only visible sign that he hadn't gone to sleep while leaning against one of the tent poles—and then she tossed all four cards into the air. He responded so fluidly and smoothly that, unless you checked out the results, it seemed he was moving much more slowly than he was—but the results were the same as always: four rapid-fire shots, right through the middle of the four cards.

The next trick was one I never liked to watch. The Dancer tied the girl onto a huge wheel, put a card in each of her hands, and started spinning the wheel until it was going so fast that she became little more than a blur. He turned his back on her, walked about forty feet away, pulled out a pair of knives, and displayed them to the audience. Then he spun around and hurled them toward her, releasing one no more than half a second ahead of the other. The audience gasped, and one woman let out a shriek, but each knife found its mark, pinning the cards to the spokes of the wheel. The Dancer tipped his hat and bowed deeply, looking slightly unhappy as he always did, and then prepared for his next trick. It involved shooting a cigarette out of the girl's mouth, and I decided that I didn't want to watch it, so I went over to the strip show.

Gloria was just being introduced as Butterfly Delight, and the customers—95 percent of them male—gave her a rousing hand. When it became apparent that she was going to do nothing but a striptease and would wind up pretty much the way the other girls started out the applause stopped, but Gloria was oblivious to the disappointed muttering. She bumped and she ground and she dipped and she teased as if she were following Ann Corio or Gypsy Rose Lee fifty years ago. I was afraid they would boo her off the stage—I was *always* afraid they would boo her off the stage—but this time was no different from any of the others. A few of them appreciated the work that had gone into her routine, and most of them settled down to wait for the next act. I hoped it wasn't Stogie: when you play as raw as we do, I wouldn't want to be the comic who had to keep the marks amused for ten minutes right after Gloria had tried to put a little class into the meat show.

I left the tent and walked up and down the Midway, checking out the games. Diggs had fired a couple of his clumsier helpers and put two fast-talking young men in their places, and business was booming—as booming as business can get in Vermont in the fall, anyway. The Rigger himself was having trouble getting customers to shell out at one of the booths, and since I hadn't made an appearance on the Midway since we arrived, I decided to help him out. I caught his eye, and a moment later he started teasing and taunting me until I finally agreed to play the game. I won two hundred dollars in about five minutes, and managed to pass the money back to one of the shills as the marks all crowded around the booth, hot to play a game that even a retarded hunchback could win.

I heard Thaddeus' voice over the loudspeaker and I knew it was time to get back to the sideshow. When I arrived I learned that Snoopy—the Dog-Faced Boy—had collapsed while I was gone. He claimed it was due to stomach cramps, but Mr. Ahasuerus thought it was the cumulative effect of our gravity, which evidently was much stronger than any he had been used to.

We kept it from Thaddeus as long as we could, but finally I had to tell him that Snoopy wouldn't be able to work. I had been afraid that he would throw a tantrum right in front of the customers, but he simply shook his head disgustedly and went on with his spiel.

When the last show was over he walked back to the dormitory tent with me to have a look at Snoopy for himself. The Dog-Faced Boy was panting heavily and drooling all over himself, and there wasn't any question that he was in serious discomfort.

"Well?" said Thaddeus, turning to Mr. Ahasuerus.

"I can't be sure," said the Blue Man, "but I think it has been caused by your gravity."

"Then why didn't he get sick sooner?"

"For the same reason that you don't die during the first few seconds that you are submerged in water."

"Are you trying to tell me that he's dying?" demanded Thaddeus.

"No. But he needs rest. His body has been under tremendous stress."

"How much rest?"

"A day, a week, a month," said the Blue Man. "Who can say?"

"*I* can," replied Thaddeus. "He works tomorrow night."

"And if he can't?"

"Then he's going to find out what bodily stress is all about!" promised Thaddeus.

He walked to the center of the tent, and emitted a loud shrill whistle.

"This has got to stop!" he announced when he had everyone's attention. "Unless you want to be locked up in cages between one show and the next, and fed nothing but dog food and water, Snoopy had damned well better be the last one to get sick." He turned his head slowly, staring at each alien in turn. "I'm not kidding," he said at last. "If one more of you gets sick or pretends to get sick or tries to convince me that he's sick, everyone is going to suffer."

He stalked over to one of the tables we had set up and told me to bring him a cup of coffee.

"They really *are* sick, Thaddeus," I told him when I returned. "These are aliens. They weren't meant to live here."

"Nobody made them come," he said irritably.

"But *you're* making them stay," I pointed out.

"Don't you go putting the blame on me, you little dwarf!" he snapped. "*I* didn't fly halfway across the galaxy. They took their chances, and they lost."

"Then you're really going to lock them up if one of them gets sick?"

"I told them I would," he said. "Why should you doubt it?"

"It wouldn't be the first time you said something you didn't mean," I answered.

"Just how the hell many things can I back down on? These bastards get the idea that I can be pushed around and pretty soon they'll be putting you and me on exhibit on the moon."

I could see that talking to him wasn't going to do any good, so I fell silent for a while. Then Thaddeus sent me over to his trailer for a six-pack of beer, and when I returned he spent the next two hours nursing one beer after another, shooting an occasional contemptuous glance in the direction of Dapper Dan.

Finally he went off to his trailer, and after I found out that Mr. Ahasuerus had organized the healthy aliens into an around-the-clock nursing team, I broke down and followed him. I didn't relish sharing quarters with Thaddeus, even if he didn't have a woman in for the night, but I had been sleeping on canvas cots for almost two weeks and it wasn't doing my back any good. I've never been really comfortable ever since my spine started twisting, but I couldn't remember it ever hurting more than when I'd wake up after a night on one of the canvas cots.

"Well, look who's here," said Thaddeus when I walked into the trailer. "I kind of thought you wouldn't be showing up here again."

"Back problems," I said.

"To say nothing of stench problems," he said with a grimace. "My God, that Pumpkin stinks, doesn't she?"

"It's the rash," I said. "We don't have anything we can treat it with."

"If they're all this puny, I think Man is going to conquer the whole damned universe ten years after he develops something that'll get him from one star to the next," said Thaddeus. "I've never seen a sicklier bunch of creatures in my life."

"Take a batch of humans to one of their worlds, and you might," I said.

He shrugged. "Maybe you're right."

He was going to say something more, but just then there was a knock on the door.

"It's open!" shouted Thaddeus.

I heard the door open and shut, and then Alma walked into the room, wearing a heavy sweater and a pair of

85

faded jeans. Thaddeus looked surprised for just a moment, and then his face became a blank.

"May I sit down?" she asked.

He gestured toward a chair.

"Thank you. Thaddeus, I have to talk to you."

"I'd better leave," I said, getting up from the couch, but Thaddeus pushed me back down.

"Stick around, Tojo," he said. "This is *your* trailer, too."

"I'd rather we spoke alone," she said uneasily.

"I'm sure you would," said Thaddeus. "But we no longer have any intimate secrets, do we? Unless you have some new ones to tell me, that is."

"You're making this very difficult for me, Thaddeus," said Alma.

"I can't imagine why," he said bitterly. "We don't have all that much in common anymore, so why should a little talk be difficult?"

"I stopped by the tent tonight," she said.

"Oh?" replied Thaddeus, lighting a cigarette. "Which tent?"

"You know which tent," she said. "Is it true?"

"Probably. But just for the record, is *what* true?"

"Are you really going to put them in Monk's cages if another one of them gets sick?"

"Why should it concern you?" he said.

"You didn't answer me," said Alma.

"You noticed," he said with a harsh grin. "Why don't you ask Queenie? I understand she has all the answers these days."

"Are you going to put Rainbow on display if Dapper Dan doesn't go on tomorrow?"

"You'd better believe it!" snapped Thaddeus. "Being sick is one thing. Going on strike is another."

"Can't you see that Dapper Dan is the sickest of them all?" she said.

"He's as healthy as I am," said Thaddeus.

"Physically, yes. But he thinks he's going to die, and that you've condemned his soul to everlasting perdition."

"Who told you that?" demanded Thaddeus, suddenly tense.

"Mr. Ahasuerus."

"Did he say what religion Dapper Dan practices?"

"I don't know," said Alma. "Probably some Eastern one. What difference does it make? He thinks you're sending him to hell. That's all that matters."

I could see the tension seep away from him as he realized that she still thought they were merely freaks: odd and ill-formed, but of this world.

"What do you want me to do?" he asked at last. "Close down the show every time one of them wishes he was somewhere else?"

She shook her head. "Just treat them like human beings. They may be different, Thaddeus, but they're not monsters. You've got to start allowing them their dignity."

"Well, now, look who's talking about dignity!" said Thaddeus, a cruel grin on his face. "You spread your legs to two thousand strange men every day and then you go home and crawl into the sack with a dumpy fifty-five-year-old broad who didn't even know which side of her welfare check to sign when I found her. That's some god-damned dignity!"

"Who taught me to work in a meat show?" said Alma without any hint of anger. "As for Queenie, she loves me."

"Hah!" snorted Thaddeus.

"She does, Thaddeus. I'm important to her. She treats me like a person instead of just a body. You treated me like you treat *them*. You can't go through your whole life using people like that. It's got to stop!"

She pulled a crumpled Kleenex out of her pocket and blew her nose.

"I didn't mean to lecture you, Thaddeus," she said slowly. "It never does any good, and it's not what I came over for."

"Now that you're on the subject, just what the hell *are* you doing here, besides telling me how to run my business?"

"I've come to make a deal," she said. "You like deals, don't you?"

"I'm listening."

She shifted uneasily on her chair and lowered her gaze to the floor. "If you'll promise not to put them in cages, or to make Rainbow work in the sideshow until he's healthy, I'll move back in with you."

I don't know what Thaddeus was expecting, but that

sure wasn't it. For just a second he looked surprised; then a strange expression—perhaps concern, perhaps something else—crossed his face.

"Did you have a fight with Queenie?" he asked after a long, uncomfortable pause.

"No," said Alma, still staring at the floor.

"Does she know you're making this offer?"

Alma shook her head, and a tear trickled down her cheek.

"Do you love her?" he asked softly.

"I need her. I need *someone*," she whispered, more tears following the first.

"And you're offering to come back, just because of a bunch of freaks?"

She forced herself to look at him. "Is it a deal?" she asked, her face very pale and very wet.

"I'd make you unhappy."

"You always do."

"I'd still sleep with other women," he said. "I'm too old to change."

"I know," she replied, blowing her nose again.

"Queenie would hate you even more than she hates me," he pointed out. "If you move in here, she'll never take you back. She's not as generous as I am."

"Queenie will live without me. Those poor creatures won't."

"You really think I'd kill them?"

"You kill everything you touch in one way or another," said Alma, never taking her eyes from his. "This won't be any worse for me than working in the show."

"Or any better?" he asked with a wry smile.

"Or any better."

"And yet," he said, truly puzzled, "you'd come back. For *them*."

"Yes." She wiped the tears from her face with a forearm. "You know something, Thaddeus?" she said with a wistful little smile. "When I was nine or ten years old I was one hell of a tomboy. I played football and baseball with the best of them, and I used to go home with cuts and bruises all over me, but I never cried—not once." She ran the soggy Kleenex over her face. "Until I met you."

He stared at her and said nothing. I think she must

88

have felt more naked than she ever felt on any stage, and she began shifting uncomfortably again.

"Well?" she asked at last, and her voice shook just a little. "Do we have a deal?"

"Go back where you belong," he said wearily. It could have sounded nasty, but somehow it didn't.

"What?" she asked, blinking as if she was sure she hadn't understood him.

"Go back to Queenie."

"You don't want me?" she said, a blush of shame starting to spread across her face.

"I don't make deals."

She turned to me, and I could tell she was going to start crying again. "Goodnight, Tojo. I'm sorry you had to hear this."

"Goodnight, Alma," I said. "Take care."

She turned and walked out of the trailer without saying another word.

"She really thought I was going to lock them in cages," said Thaddeus, watching her through a window as she ran to Queenie's trailer.

"Weren't you?" I said.

"With everything I've done, she was willing to come back for more, just to help them," he said, ignoring my question. "Isn't that odd?"

He lit another cigarette and looked at the dormitory tent for a long minute.

"It's starting to snow again," he said.

"I know," I replied.

"Tojo," he said in a faraway voice, "get your ass over there and tell Rainbow he'd better stay in bed tomorrow. It looks like it's going to be a cold day."

He was still staring at the tent when I left the trailer to do his bidding.

10.

At three o'clock the next morning Dapper Dan tried to kill himself.

Big Alvin pounded on the door to the trailer until he finally woke us up. He was standing there in only his T-shirt and jeans, totally oblivious to the snow and wind, and screaming that Thaddeus had to get over to the dormitory tent right away.

As always when there was an emergency concerning the carnival, Thaddeus was up and dressed and reasonably wide awake in less than a minute. I can't move as fast as most people, and it took me about three minutes just to get out of my pajamas and into my clothes, and another minute or so to reach the tent. When I entered it Thaddeus was already working on the Missing Link, who was weakly trying to push him away.

"Mustard!" he snapped at Alvin. The big guy just stood there with an uncomprehending look on his face. "Dammit, Alvin! Get me a jar of mustard!"

"Any particular kind?" asked Big Alvin.

"Just get it, you dumb son of a bitch!" bellowed Thaddeus.

Alvin shrugged and went out the door, obviously on his way to one of the concession stands. I walked over to Queenie's kitchen, found a bottle of yellow mustard, and brought it to Thaddeus.

He took it from me without a word and poured half its contents into Dapper Dan's mouth. The Missing Link fought against it, but finally swallowed the stuff.

"Stand back!' Thaddeus ordered the other aliens, who had all crowded around. "Give him air!"

A moment later Dapper Dan clutched his belly, and a few seconds after that he began vomiting. Thaddeus, a disgusted look on his face, held the apeman's head until he was finished.

"Don't just stand there, Treetop!" he hollered. "Get something to clean this up with."

He turned to me. "Do you know what that bastard did? He took a whole bottle of Four-Eye's sodium pills. Swallowed every last one of them." He put a hand on Dapper Dan's shoulder and looked down at him. "You poor dumb monkeyman. If you want to kill yourself, you don't announce that you've taken the pills until they've had time to get into your system. Now all you're gonna have is one hell of a bellyache." He took the edge off his voice. "Are you feeling any better?"

Dapper Dan made no answer.

"*Would* the sodium have killed him?" I asked dubiously.

"Who knows?" responded Thaddeus wearily. "I think fresh air and sunshine would kill half of them. For all I know his standard diet is bird shit."

"I will try again," said Dapper Dan softly.

"I don't doubt it," said Thaddeus.

Dapper Dan looked up at him. "Why couldn't you let me die?"

"Maybe next time I will," said Thaddeus.

"I hope so," said Dapper Dan.

"Jesus Christ, what the hell's the matter with you?" snapped Thaddeus. "You're getting fed, you're not being beaten, there's always a chance that Romany will find you. What the hell do you want to die for?"

"Leave him alone, Thaddeus," I said.

"Let me tell you something, Tarzan," he continued, ignoring me completely. "If it was me instead of you, I'd have made twenty escape attempts already. I'd be lying in wait for you every time you walked into the tent. I'd *go* on a hunger strike instead of just threatening to. It doesn't take any brains or guts to kill yourself—or maybe it does, considering how badly you botched it. What kind of people are you, anyway?"

Dapper Dan looked as if he was going to say something, but suddenly tried to vomit again. Nothing came up, and he finally lay back, exhausted, on his cot.

"Just lie still and try to relax," said Thaddeus, picking up a towel and mopping the Missing Link's face. "You start moving around and you'll start heaving again.

There's been enough stupidity around here for one night."

"Please go away," said Dapper Dan softly.

"When I'm ready to," replied Thaddeus. He sat down on the edge of the cot and took Dapper Dan's pulse. "I wish I knew what the hell was normal for you," he said after a moment or two. Then he reached into his pocket and pulled out a cigarette, lit it, and took a long drag. "That must be some world you come from, apeman."

"What do you mean?" whispered Dapper Dan.

"Well, you'd rather kill yourself than stay away from it."

"I would rather die than remain in bondage," said Dapper Dan.

"That's an interesting conclusion to reach in less than two weeks. Don't they have any jails on your world?"

"No."

"You're kidding!" scoffed Thaddeus. "What do you do when someone breaks the law?"

"No one does," said Dapper Dan.

"I don't believe you."

"What you believe is of no importance to me."

"Other than the freedom to pretend you're a sideshow freak for Ahasuerus instead of really being one for me," said Thaddeus, "just what *is* important to you?"

"My family and my God," said Dapper Dan.

"In that order?"

"There is no order. They are the same."

"Ancestor worship?"

Dapper Dan shook his head weakly. "You would not understand."

"Try me."

"To what purpose? Whether I die now or I die later, I must search for my God alone."

"You make it sound like he's lost," said Thaddeus with a smile.

"God is not lost," said Dapper Dan so softly that I had trouble hearing him. "But *I* am."

"What the hell do you mean by that?" asked Thaddeus.

Dapper Dan merely closed his eyes and turned on his side.

"I heard him speak about it earlier this evening," I said. "As I understand it, he believes his soul will be lost if he dies without the sacraments of his religion."

"Is that right?" said Thaddeus thoughtfully.

"He was very distressed at the thought of dying away from home," I said.

"So he tries to kill himself rather than take the chance that he might die here sometime in the future," said Thaddeus. "That's about as logical as these jokers get."

"He's been pretty depressed, Thaddeus," I said. "I don't think he's thinking very clearly."

"Well," said Thaddeus, a puzzled frown crossing his face, "he seems to be clear on one point." He touched Dapper Dan gently on the shoulder. "You'd really rather go to hell for all eternity than spend another day here?"

"Yes!" howled the Missing Link.

His huge hairy body was wracked by sobs, and Thaddeus suddenly stood up like he'd been shot through with electricity. For just a moment he looked like he had no idea what to do next. Then his cigarette burned down to his fingers, he cursed and threw it on the ground and snuffed it out with his shoe, and the moment was gone.

"I think he's wigged out," he said, staring at the huge alien weeping out his misery. He walked over to one of the tables and sat down at it. "Between Alma and the monkeyman, this has been a very enlightening evening," he said caustically. "Tojo, get me a cup of coffee."

While I was preparing it, Mr. Ahasuerus walked over to Thaddeus and awkwardly seated himself on a chair that was much too small for him.

"He *will* try again," said the blue man.

"It doesn't make any sense," said Thaddeus. "If he's afraid to die away from home, killing himself is about the last thing he should be considering."

"He won't do it because it is sensible," said Mr. Ahasuerus. "He has been in a severe depression."

I arrived with the coffee.

"Thanks," said Thaddeus. He turned to the blue man. "You want a cup?"

"No, thank you."

"Has Dapper Dan got a particular friend in this bunch, someone who could talk a little sense to him?" asked Thaddeus. "I can have him watched twenty-four hours a day, but it would be a lot easier on all of us if I didn't have to."

"He spent a lot of time speaking with the Human Liz-

93

ard and the Sphinx on the voyage to Earth," offered Mr. Ahasuerus.

"Tojo," said Thaddeus, "get Numa and Albert over here."

I sought out the two aliens. Numa refused to speak with Thaddeus, but Albert followed me to the table.

"Your friend Dapper Dan has gone off the deep end," said Thaddeus, as the Human Lizard took a seat.

"I don't understand."

"He's become irrational."

"Why?" hissed Albert the Alligator. "Because he doesn't like slavery?"

"Because he tried to kill himself," said Thaddeus patiently. "And I gather that according to his beliefs, this is not exactly the best way to enjoy a happy afterlife."

"He's going to die on your world anyway," said Albert in his distinct and sibilant whisper. "Why not get it over with as soon as possible, so that he can begin searching for his deity immediately?"

"You're as crazy as he is!" snapped Thaddeus in exasperation.

"Because I see nothing wrong in his killing himself to avoid a lifetime of degradation?" hissed Albert.

"If it's such a tempting alternative, why haven't you tried it?" said Thaddeus.

"Because my situation is different," answered Albert. "This experience, distasteful as it is, constitutes only the smallest portion of my lifetime. I shall be alive centuries after you are nothing but an unpleasant memory."

Thaddeus shot Mr. Ahasuerus a quick look, and the blue man nodded.

"How comforting," said Thaddeus dryly. "I don't suppose all those years of experience you've piled up might give you a hint about Dapper Dan's situation?"

"His situation is intolerable," said Albert, staring unblinking at Thaddeus with his cold lifeless eyes. "It will remain intolerable until you release him."

"That wasn't exactly the answer I had in mind," said Thaddeus. "Can't you speak to him, tell him about the glories of his home world and of all the wonderful things that await him there?"

"There is nothing wonderful about his planet," hissed the Human Lizard.

"Maybe not to a refugee from the Reptile House," said Thaddeus, "but it must be a desirable place for him."

"I doubt it," said Albert. "It is a world of bitter extremes of climate and a totalitarian theocracy."

"That he believes in," said Thaddeus.

"Believing in his religion makes it no less oppressive," said Albert emotionlessly.

"Then talk to him about his family, about how much they'll miss him."

"They won't," replied Albert.

"What are you talking about?"

"He is an outcast."

Thaddeus turned to Mr. Ahasuerus. "How the hell did you put this group together—empty the jails and the loony bins?"

"I know nothing about this," said Mr. Ahasuerus.

"Suppose you enlighten us," said Thaddeus, turning back to the Human Lizard.

"He became an outcast when he elected to come here," said Albert. "The moment he missed his daily religious sacrament he ceased to exist to his family."

"Then why the hell did he come?" demanded Thaddeus.

"Had he returned he would have done certain penances—hideous penances, even by *your* standards—and he would have been exonerated. But until that occurs, he might as well be dead as far as his friends and family are concerned. Indeed, he is less than dead to them."

"And he accepted that just to set foot on a little ball of shit spinning around a distant sun?" said Thaddeus uncomprehendingly. He turned to me. "He must be one unhappy monkeyman."

"He is," I said softly.

"I wonder what he thought he'd find here?" mused Thaddeus.

"Something other than what he found," hissed Albert coldly.

"How about you?" said Thaddeus, seemingly anxious to change the subject. "Why are *you* here?"

"I am an exobiologist."

"A *what*?"

"My life's work is the study of alien life forms. I was

presented with an opportunity to visit a planet I had never been to before. I took it."

"You mean you could have told us right off the bat why some of you were getting sick and how to cure you?" demanded Thaddeus.

"Probably."

"Then why the hell didn't you?"

"Most of them, like the Missing Link, would be better off dead," said Albert.

"Yeah?" said Thaddeus. "Well, I just hope you're as unhappy as *he* is."

"Why?"

"I don't like you very much," said Thaddeus. "I don't like your looks, and I don't like the way you speak, and I don't like your attitude."

"Have you considered how your attitude might appear to one of us?" asked Albert.

Thaddeus glared at him for a long moment. "We're getting off the subject," he said at last. "Will you speak to him?"

"I will not."

"And you?" he said, looking at Mr. Ahasuerus.

"I will try," replied the blue man. "He is my responsibility."

"Good," said Thaddeus, rising to his feet. "Hey, Alvin!"

The big guy hurried over.

"Alvin, keep a close eye on Dapper Dan for the next couple of days. If you have to tie him down to keep him from trying to off himself, do it. And have Queenie tell Gloria to go to town tomorrow for more sodium pills."

Alvin nodded, and Thaddeus walked over to the Missing Link. He didn't say a word, just stood and looked at him. Dapper Dan was asleep now, breathing deeply and regularly, but his face was troubled, as if he were having a bad dream. Thaddeus reached out a hand as if he was going to give the Missing Link a reassuring pat on the shoulder; when his hand got halfway to its mark he suddenly drew back.

"Come on, Tojo!" he snapped. "There's no sense hanging around here. Everything's back to normal."

I followed him to the trailer. Neither of us was sleepy, so he opened a pair of beers and handed one to me.

Jupiter Monk entered as we were drinking them in silence.

"Hope you don't mind the intrusion," he said, rubbing his hands and blowing on them, "but old Alvin woke the whole place up a few minutes ago looking for mustard, of all things, and since I saw your light on I thought—"

"Stop jabbering and grab yourself a beer," said Thaddeus.

"I thought you'd never ask," grinned Monk, walking to the refrigerator. "Ah, I see you've switched from bottles to cans."

"It's what they had," replied Thaddeus with a shrug.

Monk popped open a can and joined us in the living room.

"Man, it's a bitch of a night, isn't it?" he said. "Reminds me of the Klondike, except up there we didn't have anything to worry about except polar bears and wolves and maybe an occasional moose."

"So what's down here?" I asked.

"Cops. Marks. Rubes. Thaddeus. For safety, I'll take the Klondike every time."

"What's that supposed to mean?" said Thaddeus irritably.

"Well, you got to admit you ain't always as easy to get along with as a polar bear," laughed Monk.

"If you've come here to dump on me you can go right back where you came from," said Thaddeus. "I've had enough people telling me what they think of me for one night."

"As a matter of fact, I came over because I finally came up with our last name."

"What are you talking about?"

"The Three-Breasted Woman," said Monk. "We never could decide on a name for her."

"And now you've got one?"

"Yep."

"Just how many hours did you spend thinking about it?" said Thaddeus sarcastically.

"Came to me in a flash," said Monk.

"So what is it?"

"I figure each of those breasts is a D-cup," said Monk, a pleasant smile crossing his face as he pictured them in

97

his mind's eye, "and she's got three of them, so how about 3-D?"

"It's awful!" snorted Thaddeus. "It sounds like a movie gimmick."

"You got anything better?"

He didn't, and no one came up with anything better, so she became 3-D, and the whole troupe finally had carny names.

We had a few more beers, and then Monk looked at his watch and discovered that it was almost five-thirty.

"I'd better go," he said, draining the can he was holding in his hand. "If I hurry, my head'll hit the pillow before my alarm clock goes off." He glanced out the window. "Shit! It's snowing again. What the hell did you leave California for, Thaddeus? You must have been crazy."

Thaddeus merely shrugged.

"Where were you—north or south?"

"South," said Thaddeus. "A suburb of L.A."

"Anaheim?"

"Santa Cruz."

"Too bad it wasn't Anaheim," said Monk. "They've got the Angels and Disneyland and all kinds of good things."

"We were just a few miles away," said Thaddeus.

Monk put his coat on and buttoned it up. "We ain't either of us too smart. I could be hunting apes in Africa, and you could be watching a batch of 2-Ds shaking on a California beach." He opened the door. "See you tomorrow."

"Close that damned thing!" shouted Thaddeus. "It's freezing!"

Monk laughed and slammed the door behind him as he went out into the snow.

Thaddeus opened another beer and offered one to me.

"No, thanks," I said.

"Have one," he said, pushing it into my hand. "I don't like to drink alone."

"Thaddeus," I said slowly, "where *did* you grow up?"

"What difference does it make?"

"None. But I know where Santa Cruz is: it's a suburb of San Francisco."

"Big deal."

"But I thought you said——"

"How the hell do I know where Santa Cruz is?" he snapped. "I heard it mentioned in a movie."

"You didn't grow up there?"

"I've never been to California in my life," he said bitterly.

We sat, silent and motionless, for perhaps ten minutes while the wind whipped against the windows and the snow kept accumulating.

"I was born in Trenton, New Jersey," he said at last. "My mother was the cheapest whore in town. Even the black guys wouldn't touch her. She got nothing but freaks and winos."

"And your father?" I asked gently.

"There isn't a hat big enough to pull his name out of," said Thaddeus, his voice low and toneless. "I grew up in a one-room flat, watching my mother fuck two hundred, three hundred men a week and shoot every cent she made into her goddamned arm. The state kept taking me away and putting me in foster homes, and I kept coming back. Until I was twelve."

"What happened then?"

"Some junkie bashed her head in. I found her after he had gone."

"Then what did you do?"

"A little of everything." He looked out the window. "Mostly I starved and I froze. California girls—hah! I've never been halfway to the Mississippi."

"Then why say you did?" I asked. "No one in a carny cares where you came from."

"*I* care," he said so softly I could hardly hear him. "I spent my whole fucking life fighting and clawing for every penny so that I'd never wind up back in that goddamned room in Trenton."

"But why California?"

"Because it's clean," he said. "I like to tell myself that one time in my life I was someplace that was clean." He turned to me suddenly. "If it's dirty, I don't want to hear about it."

"It's clean, Thaddeus," I lied.

He finished his beer. "If you ever tell anyone what I just said, I'm gonna rip that goddamned hump off your back and shove it down your throat," he said. "You got that straight, you fucking dwarf?"

"I won't tell anyone, Thaddeus," I said.

"You'd better not," he muttered, and lay down on the couch. He was asleep in less than a minute, and as I looked at him, curled up in the same position as Dapper Dan and with the same unhappy expression on his face, I was struck by how little difference there was between the two of them.

I noticed that it was cold inside the trailer, so I covered him with a blanket, as I had done so many times in the past, and went off to my own bed. As I lay down and prepared to go to sleep, I found myself wondering what Dapper Dan's mother had done for a living, or if he had thought of this world as *his* California.

11.

I woke Thaddeus up at noon. He had his usual hangover, he was his usual irritable self, and he croaked for his usual cup of coffee.

"Thanks," he said when I brought it to him. He took a sip, warmed his hands on the mug, and closed his eyes. "Better," he muttered. "That was some night we had last night, wasn't it?" he said with a wry smile. "Alma being noble, of all things, and the monkeyman trying to kill himself, and . . ."

His voice trailed off, and I could tell by the troubled expression on his face that he remembered what he had confided to me. Suddenly he became very ill at ease, almost ashamed; it was a new posture for Thaddeus, and while I had waited for it for years I had to admit to myself that it didn't become him.

He finished his coffee in silence, dressed quickly, and walked across the Midway to the dormitory tent. I cleaned up the kitchen and made the beds, and by the time I followed him over he was sitting on the edge of Dapper Dan's cot, examining his pulse and heartbeat as if he knew normal from abnormal.

Then he called for a cup of soup. Queenie brought it over, and Thaddeus started spooning it out to Dapper Dan. The fight seemed to be out of the Missing Link—if "fight" was the right word for it in the first place—and he swallowed each spoonful as Thaddeus gave it to him.

When the bowl was empty Thaddeus turned to Big Alvin and Treetop, who had been standing guard since before the suicide attempt.

"Didn't anyone think that maybe he could use a little food?" he demanded. "Hell, he puked until he didn't have anything left inside of him."

Neither of the men answered him, and Thaddeus called Mr. Ahasuerus over.

"How about you?" he said. "I thought he was supposed to be your responsibility."

"I thought rest was more important than nourishment," said the blue man.

"Nobody's paying you to think!" snapped Thaddeus. "Hell, it's freezing in here! He needs calories more than he needs sleep!"

He stomped around the tent, full of impotent rage. Finally he wound up back at Dapper Dan's cot.

"You!" he said sharply. "If I move you to my trailer, will you give me your word that you won't try to kill yourself or try to escape?"

"No," said Dapper Dan, staring weakly but unblinking at Thaddeus.

Thaddeus stared back at him for a long moment, then turned to the guards again. "Alvin, you and Treetop rig up a stretcher out of one of the cots and move him to the trailer. Then tell Swede to set up housekeeping there and keep an eye on him."

"Thank you," said Mr. Ahasuerus.

Thaddeus' eyes fell on Rainbow, whose color was once again pale blue.

"This one too," he said, gesturing to the Man of Many Colors.

"Do you want us to bring them back at show time?" asked Big Alvin.

"No. They stay there until they're healthy. And Pumpkin and Snoopy stay in the tent today. Four-Eyes too, unless Gloria gets back with his pills in time."

"I could go on in their place," suggested Mr. Ahasuerus.

Thaddeus uttered a dry laugh. "I can't figure you out," he admitted. "Why the hell would you want to do me a favor?"

"I don't," replied Mr. Ahasuerus. "I simply want to make sure that you don't lose so much money that you must force any of my sick companions back into the sideshow before they are ready."

"Don't worry about it," said Thaddeus. "They're not worth anything to me if they're dead."

"Very well," said Mr. Ahasuerus. "I withdraw my offer."

"Your withdrawal is accepted."

"May I ask a question?"

"Go right ahead," said Thaddeus, lighting up a cigarette and offering one to the blue man, who refused it.

"Since you . . . ah . . . took over the management of the sideshow, you have never once displayed me to the public."

"Are you feeling slighted?" asked Thaddeus.

"Merely curious."

"Good. It'll give you food for thought," replied Thaddeus.

"That is the only answer I am to be given?" asked Mr. Ahasuerus.

"It is."

The blue man looked at him, puzzled. Then he shrugged and walked away.

"I've been wondering about that myself, Thaddeus," I said.

He lowered his voice until none of the others could hear it. "Simple. You give their leader special privileges, even if he doesn't ask for them, or want them, and you get them to thinking about it, and they may be a little less likely to follow him when he tries to take over."

"You think he's going to try something, then?"

"Of course."

"But he's been more cordial and cooperative than just about anyone else would be in the same circumstances," I protested.

"Tojo, the man works for a corporation, just like anyone else. And he must be pretty high up the ladder to have a spaceship and a bunch of tourists from other worlds entrusted to him. What does that imply to you?"

"What *should* it imply?" I asked.

"Nobody reaches a position of authority without the ability to be a back-stabbing bastard when the chips are down. I don't know why he's trying to soften me up, but it doesn't make any difference. If he's the leader, then he's got to be the toughest of them."

"But he's not a human being," I said, not even remarking on the fact that Thaddeus had, for the first time, referred to him as a *man*. "Maybe things are different on his world."

"As near as I can tell, there's one basic law anywhere you go in the universe: the strong eat the weak."

"I think you're wrong," I said. "I hope you are."

"What if I am? There's no harm done, and at least he doesn't have to put up with all the hicks staring at him. And if I'm right . . ." He let his voice trail off and flashed a smile at me.

⋆ The replacements for Treetop and Big Alvin showed up just then, and Thaddeus broke away to start directing the removal of Dapper Dan and Rainbow to the trailer. Then it was show time, and he marched the six healthy aliens—Gloria hadn't come back with Four-Eyes' pills yet—onto their platforms.

Since it was even colder in the sideshow tent than the dormitory tent, I decided to fill a number of cups with coffee and carry them around to the exhibits on a tray. I had just handed one to Bullseye and was about to offer a cup to 3-D when I saw a tall, well-dressed man with piercing eyes and an aquiline nose standing at the back of the crowd. I had only seen him once before in my life, but Mr. Romany wasn't the kind of man one could forget in a dozen lifetimes.

Thaddeus had just finished describing Stretch and his totally fictional origin to the crowd, and while they were all busy gaping at him, I walked up and tugged at Thaddeus' sleeve.

"What's up?" he asked.

"He's here!" I whispered. "He's found us!"

"Are you surprised?" he said with a smile.

"What are you going to do?" I asked.

"Finish showing off the exhibits," he replied easily. "Don't worry about Romany—he's not going to make a scene in front of a crowd."

Thaddeus went right back into his patter, and it was another fifteen minutes before he finally ushered the crowd out. Mr. Romany was last in line, and after everyone else had left he stopped just short of the doorway and turned to Thaddeus.

"You have done a very foolish thing, Mr. Flint," he said.

"Foolishness is in the eye of the beholder," replied Thaddeus with a grin. "Now, if it was me, I'd say that walking alone into the enemy's camp was pretty damned foolish."

"Are you trying to frighten me?" asked Mr. Romany, cocking an eyebrow and looking mildly amused.

"Perish the thought," said Thaddeus. "Just making an observation. What are you doing here?"

"You know perfectly well what I'm doing here," said Mr. Romany. "I want them back."

"I don't doubt it," replied Thaddeus with a chuckle.

"Well?"

"This is neither the time nor the place to talk about it."

"This is precisely the time and the place," said Mr. Romany.

"Use your brain," said Thaddeus. "It's in both of our interests to keep what's going on a secret. There are too many people passing through here."

"How about your office?"

"Out of the question. There's a bar in town called Lucy's Tavern. Meet me there in an hour."

"How do I know you'll show up?" asked Mr. Romany suspiciously.

"You don't," answered Thaddeus. "But you do know I can't move the show in less than a day, so you can always come back here and find me."

Mr. Romany seemed to be considering it. "Why must we go into town? Why not speak here, on the grounds?"

"Because I don't want your telepathic friend anywhere around when we talk."

"Then you know about him?"

"Of course I know about him," said Thaddeus. "Who the hell do you think you're dealing with?"

Mr. Romany consulted his wristwatch. "One hour," he said, and walked out of the sideshow tent.

"See?" Thaddeus said to me. "Nothing to it."

"It's not over," I replied.

"You still don't understand how the game is played, do you?" he said with a smile. "He wanted to talk now. I made him back down. He wanted to talk here. I made him go into town. He probably wanted Bullseye around. I made him meet me alone."

"What does that prove?"

"It proves that he's operating under a lot more restraints than I am," answered Thaddeus. "And it also means that, tough as he looks, he's not going to be able to make any effective threats." He paused to clear his throat.

"Maybe I can't stop Dapper Dan from killing himself, and maybe I don't know how to make Alma happy, but Romany is a different cup of tea: we're playing in my ball park again, and I know all the ground rules. Put the freaks away and grab your jacket. You're coming with me."

"But why?"

"Because he won't want you to," said Thaddeus. "What's the good of dealing from strength if you don't play any cards?"

I escorted the six aliens back to the tent, made sure that Gloria had dropped off the sodium pills for Four-Eyes, and hunted up my jacket. I considered telling Mr. Ahasuerus that Mr. Romany had found us, but decided not to get his hopes up. (It wasn't until we were halfway to town that I realized he would know anyway: the others had to have seen and recognized Mr. Romany during the show. I spent the rest of the ride wondering if Mr. Ahasuerus would think me Thaddeus' lackey for *not* telling him.)

The town was like most northern Vermont villages: narrow streets, a huge town square, old frame buildings (mostly saltboxes, with hydra-headed chimneys) that had been converted into stores and shops, and an occasional long low office building with so much glass on display that you couldn't help wondering how they heated it when the really cold weather arrived.

Lucy's Tavern was the carny folks' hangout when they weren't working or drinking in their trailers. It was an old three-story home with tongue-in-groove paneling that boasted an undersized bar and about a dozen small tables with uncomfortable wooden chairs in what had once been the living room. Each table possessed a bowl of peanuts, provided *gratis* by the management, and the floor was littered with peanut shells, which remained where they fell, either to add to the atmosphere or because Lucy and her employees were simply disinclined to sweep them up.

It was midafternoon when we arrived, and the place was totally deserted, except for a bored-looking bartender who had his nose buried in a *National Geographic* magazine. Mr. Romany was sitting at a table in the farthest corner of the dimly lit barroom, waiting for us with a bottle of Schlitz and a half-empty glass in front of him.

Thaddeus left me at the table, ordered a couple of beers at the bar, and returned a minute later.

"I thought you were coming alone," said Mr. Romany.

"I told you once before," grinned Thaddeus. "He's my bodyguard."

Mr. Romany stared at me.

"He's small, but he's wiry," added Thaddeus. He pulled up a chair and seated himself. "Did you have a nice trip?"

"Once I got out of jail."

"View it as an occupational hazard," said Thaddeus, still smiling.

"I've endured worse."

"If you had any playing cards with you, you could have turned it into a paying proposition," said Thaddeus.

"Shall we stop the small talk and get down to the business at hand?" said Mr. Romany coldly.

"It suits me," agreed Thaddeus. "How about you, Tojo?"

"Fine," I said, startled.

"All right," said Mr. Romany. "You have committed a serious crime, Mr. Flint. Even by the rather lax standards of this planet, kidnapping is a major felony."

"Then you should report me to the police. If *you* had committed a crime, I certainly wouldn't hesitate, as you may have noticed.

"We both know that is impossible."

"Well, we're both in the same boat then, aren't we?" replied Thaddeus. "You don't want the authorities to know they're aliens, and I don't want the authorities to know I've kidnapped them. I guess we're just going to have to trust each other."

I watched Mr. Romany very closely for a reaction, but there wasn't any. Either his face was incapable of any other expression, which was certainly possible, or else he was playing his cards very close to the vest. I opted for the latter: he had known he couldn't bluff Thaddeus by invoking the authorities. He had mentioned it more as a matter of form, just to get it out of the way.

"What is to prevent me from stealing them back?" he said, and then I knew he was bluffing. He just wanted Thaddeus to outline how thoroughly he had gone about protecting the aliens to gain some insight into his antagonist.

"Not a thing," replied Thaddeus calmly. "Of course, if you do, I'll kill the Missing Link and the Man of Many Colors." He paused to let that sink in. "Check the tent if you like. You won't find them there."

"Where are they?"

"Somewhere up in Maine," lied Thaddeus. "Of course, I don't have to kill them. I might just turn them over to the government. I mean, once you've taken Mr. Ahasuerus and the rest away, I'd hardly be hurting my own income, would I?"

This time there was a reaction, a slight tightening of the muscles in Mr. Romany's lean, intent face. I knew that if I had seen it, so had Thaddeus—and he would doubtless file it away for future use. Obviously exposure meant more to Mr. Romany than the deaths of a couple of the aliens.

"You're being very unreasonable about this," said Mr. Romany at last. "You've gotten away with kidnapping, you've doubtless made a considerable amount of money because of it; now return them and no further action will be taken."

"No action has been taken at all," replied Thaddeus.

"That is due to change. The Human Pincushion is monitoring this conversation. Once he learns that you have no intention of releasing them, they will be forced to take action, with or without my help."

"Horseshit," said Thaddeus.

"I beg your pardon?"

"The Pincushion can't hear a word we're saying. All he can do is send. If he could receive, he'd have known I planned to take them over in the first place, and you'd have been a little better prepared for me. Now, Mr. Romany," he said, leaning forward on the table, "if you're all through talking nonsense, maybe we can get to the point."

"The point is that you have illegally abducted twelve sentient beings and are holding them against their wills."

"The point," said Thaddeus, "is that someone is pressuring you to clean this little problem up in a hurry. You're just a goddamned flunky, an advance man or an assistant tour guide or something like that. Someone higher

108

up is starting to worry about Mr. Ahasuerus and his group, and you don't want any black marks on your record. When promotion time rolls around, you don't want them to remember that someone had to bail you out on a little backwater world like this one."

As Thaddeus spoke Mr. Romany became more and more uncomfortable, fidgeting awkwardly in his chair.

"So the problem that confronts us now," concluded Thaddeus, a contemptuous smile on his face, "is not how we're going to save a bunch of innocent tourists from a life of bondage and degradation, but how we're going to save your ass. Would you say that about sums up the situation?"

Mr. Romany nodded unhappily.

There was a long, uncomfortable silence, during which Thaddeus flashed me an I-told-you-so grin.

"All right," he said when it became obvious that Mr. Romany was not going to speak. "You're a company man who's gummed up the works, and you don't want the company coming down on your head. I can appreciate that, and I'm sure we can work something out."

"What?" asked Mr. Romany.

"I'm not going to make any demands at all," said Thaddeus. "That would seem too much like blackmail or extortion. What you're going to do is go home, or to a motel, or wherever the hell you're staying, and see what kind of arrangement you can come up with. Then come by the carnival tomorrow at noon, and we'll talk. I'll be at Monk's bus."

"Not at the sideshow?"

"No. And if I find out you've tried to speak to Ahasuerus or any of the others, the deal's off."

Mr. Romany rose from his chair.

"One more thing," said Thaddeus.

"Yes?"

"No more bullshitting. You've got the makings of a pretty good Thaddeus Flint—but *I've* been Thaddeus Flint for thirty-four years. You understand what I'm saying?"

Mr. Romany nodded and walked out of the tavern, a far less ominous figure than when we had entered.

"Well?" Thaddeus said to me, lighting up a cigarette and downing the last of his beer.

109

"You knew all along, didn't you?" I replied.

"Tojo, when you've been in this goddamned business as long as I have, you can smell a con man at two hundred yards." He looked out the door at the retreating figure of Mr. Romany. "That goddamned son of a bitch doesn't give a shit for Ahasuerus and the others."

Just to see his reaction, I said: "Why should he?"

Thaddeus stared long and hard at me. "No reason," he said at last.

He left a few coins on the table, then walked out to the car.

"Are we going back now?" I asked.

"Soon," he said. "I want to make one stop first."

We drove around town until we came to a bookstore. Thaddeus left me in the car for a few minutes, and returned with a hardcover tucked under one arm.

"First goddamned book I've bought in ten years," he remarked, looking somewhat embarrassed.

"What's it about?" I asked.

"Astronomy."

"Any particular reason?"

"Just curious," he said.

We drove back to the carnival in silence. Thaddeus put his book in the trailer, then stopped to examine Dapper Dan.

"How's he doing?" he asked Swede.

"No problem," replied Swede. "He's pretty weak, but he doesn't seem to be getting any worse."

"Good."

"Uh—boss?" said Swede, and Thaddeus turned to him. "You want me to stick around here or to work the meat show?"

"Stick around."

"Then who'll do the meat show?" Swede persisted.

"I'll get the Rigger," said Thaddeus.

"He ain't gonna like it."

"As long as I'm the boss, he doesn't have to like it," said Thaddeus. "He just has to do it." He looked over at me. "I'd let you do it if you could."

"I know, Thaddeus," I said.

"Maybe someday when the crowds are smaller."

"It's all right, Thaddeus."

"Okay, then," he said uncomfortably. "How's Rainbow looking?"

"The same," said Swede. Rainbow was sleeping in the next room.

"Make sure he keeps covered," said Thaddeus. "Come on, dwarf; let's go to work."

We walked over to the dormitory tent and ushered the seven healthy aliens into the sideshow after making sure that Four-Eyes had taken his pills. Then Thaddeus started barking, and I went to the dormitory tent to take a nap, since I had had only a few hours sleep the night before.

I woke up around midnight, and wandered out to listen to Thaddeus' patter for the last show. He was like a jazz musician, using his words like notes, keeping the same basic themes but never quite repeating the melodies. He'd work and rework a line or a joke until he got it polished like burnished ebony, then discard it and try out a new one, and as I studied him I had the feeling that even if I could speak like normal people I still couldn't be half the barker he was. It was an art form, and you don't learn to be an artist. You're either born one, or you aren't. Somehow I knew that I wasn't.

When the show was over and we had closed up the sideshow, we escorted the aliens back to the dormitory tent. Treetop and Big Alvin were back on duty, and Treetop was standing next to Pumpkin, a glass of water in his hand.

"Come on, gorgeous," he was saying. "Just a little sip."

Pumpkin backed away from him awkwardly.

"Maybe I'll give you a little bath," he said, advancing toward her. "Christ, you smell like you could use one."

She stumbled and almost fell, and he emitted a loud guffaw.

"Not exactly the ballet type, are you?" he laughed.

He was going to say something else, but before he could, Thaddeus had grabbed him by the shoulder, spun him around, and swung a roundhouse blow toward his face. He was too tall for Thaddeus to reach his target, but he caught him on the side of the neck, and it was sufficient to knock Treetop to the ground.

"What the hell did you go and do that for?" gasped Treetop, getting to his knees and blinking rapidly.

111

"You were being paid to guard them, not tease them," said Thaddeus, his fists still doubled up.

"I was just having a little fun with her," said Treetop, rubbing his neck gingerly.

"You've got ten minutes to round up your gear and get your ass off the grounds," said Thaddeus. "If you're still here then, we're going to have Round Two."

"You're firing me for messing with a fucking freak?" said Treetop unbelievingly. "Hell, you treat 'em like shit yourself!"

"Nine minutes and counting," said Thaddeus ominously.

Treetop got groggily to his feet, shook his head in bewilderment, and walked out the door.

"Alvin," ordered Thaddeus, "keep an eye on him and make sure he leaves. If he's still hanging around here in fifteen minutes, I want to know about it."

Big Alvin nodded and left the tent, looking only slightly less puzzled than Treetop.

Thaddeus walked over to Pumpkin. "Are you all right?" he asked, and she nodded her elephantine head slowly. Then he turned to me. "Tojo, stick around until Alvin gets back."

"All right, Thaddeus," I said.

He left the tent, and Mr. Ahasuerus approached me. "I understand that Romany has found us," he said.

"I wouldn't get my hopes up if I were you," I answered. "He seems more concerned with his own situation that with yours. I was under the impression that he worked for you."

"Not exactly," said Mr. Ahasuerus, looking his disappointment. "We both work for the same employer. You don't think he'll be able to help us?"

"I don't know," I said. "He's meeting with Thaddeus again tomorrow. I'll know more then."

The blue man looked as if he was going to say something further, then changed his mind and walked back to his cot. Alvin returned about twenty minutes later to tell me that Treetop had picked up his pay from Diggs and was gone.

I stuck around for a couple of hours, then wandered over to the trailer. Dapper Dan was sleeping under Swede's watchful eye in the living room, Rainbow was

112

resting in the bedroom—and as for Thaddeus, he was sitting on the floor of the kitchen, his back propped up against the cabinets, pouring over his new book with the same single-minded intensity that was usually reserved only for his women and his profits.

12.

I woke up just before ten o'clock, as usual, and tiptoed out of the bedroom so as to not wake Rainbow. Thaddeus, totally dressed, was standing by the window in the living room, looking out at the grounds with an amused smile on his face.

"What are you doing up?" I asked.

He put a finger to his lips, pointed to Dapper Dan, who was still sound asleep, and whispered: "I haven't been to bed yet."

"Is something the matter?" I whispered back to him.

"I spent most of the night reading. When I finally looked at the time, I figured I might as well stay up or I'd oversleep my little meeting with Romany." He looked back out the window. "There's a pair of cops out there. I've been watching them for the better part of twenty minutes."

"Why are they here?"

"Why do *any* cops come to a carnival?" he smiled. "These guys must be a little new on the job, though. They don't seem to know who to talk to. I think Monk must have scared them out of a year's growth when he took Bruno out for a walk a little while ago."

I walked over to the window and looked out. The two policemen were engaged in an animated conversation with Stogie, which was always a mistake: eventually he'd tell them what they wanted to know, but not until he tried out twenty or thirty octogenarian jokes on them first. They listened to him, patiently at first, then with increasing irritation. Finally one of them shouted something at him, and after first giving them a look of complete disdain for their lack of humor or intelligence or both, he finally took his ever-present cigar out of his mouth and pointed it toward our trailer.

A moment later they knocked on the door, and Thaddeus gestured to me to follow him outside so as not to wake the two sleeping aliens.

"You're Thaddeus Flint?" asked the taller of the two cops.

"That's right," said Thaddeus, zipping his jacket up to the top and putting his hands in his pockets. "You're a little early for the show, officer."

"As a matter of fact, that's just what we want to talk to you about," was the reply.

"You don't mind if we walk while we talk, do you?" replied Thaddeus. "It's too cold to stand still."

"Fine by us," said the shorter one.

Thaddeus turned to me and nodded. It was my signal to disappear: cops didn't like witnesses around when they took payoffs.

I decided not to go back to the trailer, since I didn't want to wake the sleeping aliens, but I did stop by the Hothouse to hunt up Swede and tell him he'd better get back on duty in the next few minutes. I hung around long enough to warm up a little, then stuck my head out to see if Thaddeus was through with the police yet.

He was standing alone, lighting his first cigarette of the morning, and I walked out to join him.

"All done?" I asked.

He nodded. "Come along and keep me company, Tojo."

We walked over to the Rigger's trailer and Thaddeus pounded on the door until Diggs opened it.

"I took care of the cops," Thaddeus reported. "You're all set."

"How long?" asked the Rigger.

"Five days. Then they'll be back for more."

"Are we going to stay in this arctic wasteland for five more days?"

"I haven't decided yet," said Thaddeus. "Go back to sleep. You'll catch cold standing there in your shorts, and I might just laugh myself to death."

Diggs closed the door without another word, and we walked over to the girlie tent. Alma and three of the others were sitting around in jeans and sweaters, drinking coffee and hot chocolate laced with whiskey, while Gloria, wearing her leotards, was going through her usual morning regimen: sit-ups, kicks, leg-lifts, and stretching

115

exercises. She took her work seriously—probably *too* seriously—and I always got the feeling that the other strippers resented her, if only because she made them look so lazy by comparison.

"Good morning," said Gloria, starting to practice her shoulder shimmies.

"Nothing good about it," said Thaddeus. "It's freezing out there."

"Well?" said Alma.

"Well what?"

"I saw you talking to the cops."

"They thought it was cold too," said Thaddeus.

"Get to the point," said Alma wearily. "How strong do we have to work?"

"Pasties and G-strings."

"Okay," said Alma. "Now that you've had your joke for the day, how about it?"

"You heard me," said Thaddeus.

Gloria stopped shimmying to stare at him, and Barbara, another of the strippers, laughed sarcastically.

"Come on, Thaddeus," she said. "What's the angle?"

"There's no angle," he said gruffly. "I'm just sick and tired of paying off the cops."

"Payoff and Thaddeus go together like ham and rye," persisted Barbara. "What's coming down?"

"Not a damned thing. If you want to do a little flashing, that's up to you—but I won't bail you out."

"The freaks aren't making *that* much money," said Barbara.

"And even if they are, when did you ever turn away a fast buck with the meat show?" added Priscilla, who danced under the name of the Silicone Superstar.

"Let's have it, Thaddeus," said Barbara. "What's the bottom line?"

"The bottom line is that you broads are going to have to start working for a living instead of laying down on a stage and playing games with a bunch of hicks. If you can't hack it, you can work the games for the Rigger."

"You say it like you mean it," said Priscilla dubiously.

"I'll believe it when I see it," said Barbara.

"You'll see it starting with the first show today," said Thaddeus, "or else you're going to be out on your shapely little ass."

"You know," said Barbara, "I think you really *do* mean it." She paused uneasily for a second. "Look, Thaddeus, this is the last thing I ever thought I'd say, but . . . well, we've worked pretty strong since we've been here, and the word has to have gotten around. So if you want us to wait until we hit the next town . . ."

"You just don't listen, do you?" said Thaddeus irritably. "There are going to be two very unhappy cops sitting in the first row all week long, just looking for a reason to bust you."

"Just how much did they try to shake you down for?" asked Priscilla.

"Same as always. I just decided that I'm tired of paying for it."

"Are the freaks really pulling in that much money?"

"What the freaks are doing is none of your business," said Thaddeus. "Your business, starting here and now, is to start acting more like strippers and less like whores. If you can't remember how, watch Gloria."

"Just a minute!" said Barbara hotly. "Who made us act like that in the first place?"

"*Shut up!*" snapped Alma, who had been silent throughout, and Barbara stopped speaking, startled.

"Well," said Thaddeus, looking very uncomfortable, "that's that." He turned to me. "Come on, you lecherous little dwarf. Haven't you gotten enough of an eyeful yet?"

He walked briskly out of the tent. I fell into step behind him, but before I even got to the door Alma had run by me and grabbed Thaddeus by the arm.

"Go back inside," he said. "You'll freeze to death."

"I know how much this is going to cost you," she said, looking straight into his eyes. "Thank you."

"Don't thank me for anything," he said. "I just got goddamned sick and tired of paying off the cops."

"Did you get sick of paying them off for Rigger's games, too?"

"The Rigger's games are *his* business."

"Then thank you for being sick and tired of paying off the police." Suddenly she stood on her tiptoes, kissed him quickly and furtively on the cheek, and, looking very embarrassed, she ran back into the warmth of the tent.

"Thaddeus . . ." I began.

"Not a word, you ugly little wart!" he snapped.

We walked to the dormitory tent in silence. When we arrived he made a quick inspection of the aliens, walking among their cots and chairs. Finally he approached Mr. Ahasuerus.

"Well, what's the tally?" he asked.

"I don't understand," replied the blue man.

"Who else is sick?"

"No one."

"*That's* a surprise," he said. "How's Snoopy?"

"Much improved. He will be able to perform this afternoon."

"And Pumpkin?"

"Her improvement is somewhat less rapid," said Mr. Ahasuerus.

"But she *is* improving?"

"Yes."

Thaddeus stared at her for a minute, then sighed. "Okay. Give her the day off, Tojo."

"All right, Thaddeus," I replied.

While I was telling Pumpkin that she could remain in the dormitory tent, Barbara walked in, whispered something to Queenie, and walked right out again.

"We're going to start a little late today," Thaddeus was telling Mr. Ahasuerus as I rejoined them. "I've got a business meeting at noon."

"With Mr. Romany?"

"Not that it's any business of yours," said Thaddeus, "but yes, I'm meeting with Romany."

"Good luck," said Mr. Ahasuerus.

"Allow me to wish you the same," said Thaddeus with a sardonic smile.

"You do understand, of course, that he's only a minor functionary within the organization."

"He may be a minor functionary, but he's got a couple of major character flaws," replied Thaddeus. "I'm sure we'll be able to work something out."

"I hope so," said Mr. Ahasuerus. "I was fully as surprised as you that nobody else became sick last night. This is, when all is said and done, an alien world, and I suspect that the incidence of illness will increase dramatically in the days to come."

"Unless it's already peaked and you're all starting to

adjust to it," said Thaddeus. "Never bullshit a bullshitter, Mr. Ahasuerus."

The blue man merely shrugged and walked away. As soon as he was back among the aliens Queenie approached us.

"What now?" said Thaddeus.

"I heard what you did," she said. "And I just wanted to thank you."

"I thought you'd be just about the last person around here who'd be happy about it," he said wryly.

"Why?"

"Now you'll have to go back to work making costumes."

"It's my job," said Queenie.

"Sure. Like dancing to music is Alma's job."

"You make it very hard to thank you."

"Nobody's asking you to," he said. "I sure as hell didn't do it to make *you* happy."

"I know," replied Queenie. She looked long and hard at him. "Maybe Alma's right. Maybe there's a little more to you than meets the eye."

"Because I'm not making the girls work strong anymore?"

"Yes."

"But I'm still keeping the freaks against their will," he pointed out.

"So what? They're just freaks."

"What if I told you that one of them is a poet and another one's a biologist?"

"I wouldn't believe you," said Queenie.

"It's true."

"So what if it is? They're still freaks."

"Then why do you feed them?" he asked her.

"To feel useful," she replied honestly. "Besides, even a freak's got the right to eat."

"But not to be free, is that it?" he asked with a smile.

"Then set 'em free if that's what you want!" snapped Queenie. "Just get off my goddamned back! I'm sorry I thanked you in the first place. I only did it for Alma."

The amusement vanished from his face.

"Do you do a lot of things for Alma?"

"None of your fucking business!"

"I know it isn't, but I'd like an answer anyway," he

119

persisted awkwardly. "Is she happy with you, Queenie?"

"A damned sight happier than she was with you."

"I don't doubt it. You'd better work hard at keeping her that way."

"Is that a challenge or a threat?" demanded Queenie.

"Neither. I did my part this morning. Now you do yours."

"What are you saying?" asked Queenie, puzzled.

"I'm saying that if she's happy with you, she's yours," replied Thaddeus. "For a smart broad, Queenie, you're pretty goddamned slow on the uptake." He looked at his watch. "It's getting near time. Tojo, roust Monk out of his bus and tell him I need it for an hour or two."

He went back to say something to Mr. Ahasuerus. As I left the tent Queenie was standing there staring at him as if she still couldn't believe what she had heard. And, to be honest, I was having a little difficulty with it myself; I didn't know what was happening to Thaddeus, but I knew it couldn't have come from the cold, emotionless pages of an astronomy book.

Monk wasn't in his bus when I got there, so I hunted him up in the Hothouse and told him Thaddeus needed the bus.

"Okay," he said. "But I've got my animals in there."

"Loose?"

"Bruno's in a cage. The cats are loose. Tell him not to worry. They won't bother him."

"I think you'd better lock them up anyway," I said.

"Thaddeus knows my cats. He's not afraid of them, except maybe for the lion. How about if I just leave the leopards loose?"

"Thaddeus is having company," I explained.

"Why can't he use his own trailer for his blasted conquests?" asked Monk irritably.

"Because it's temporarily been turned into a hospital," I said. I told him about Dapper Dan and Rainbow, and finally, after much grumbling, he walked over to the bus and entered it.

"All right," he said upon emerging a minute later. "You tell him that if he busts a bedspring he's going to have a little four-legged company tonight."

"It's for a business meeting."

"Yeah? Since when has Thaddeus started paying for

it?" said Monk, vanishing back into the interior of the Hothouse.

Thaddeus joined me a few minutes later and we entered the bus. As always, the first thing I noticed was the pungent smell of cat urine, mingled with the odor of Bruno and the cats themselves. Not that the interior wasn't clean; it's just that after they'd been confined for a couple of weeks, as the weather had dictated recently, Monk usually had to scrub down the whole bus, and he simply hadn't gotten around to it yet.

There was a huge poker table covered with animal skins bolted to the floor about ten feet behind the driver's seat. Monk had pulled out the cushioned booths that had originally surrounded it after he caught Swede peeking at his cards during a poker game, and had laid in a supply of folding chairs that could be spread more equally around the table. Thaddeus opened up three of them, put them in place, and was just starting to rummage through the refrigerator for something to drink when Mr. Romany walked into the room.

"Good morning, Mr. Flint," he said, wrinkling his nose at the odor and casting a quick glance at the four caged animals.

"Have a seat," said Thaddeus. "I'll be with you in a minute." He pulled out three bottles of ginger ale, handed one to each of us, and withdrew a complicated-looking pocket knife. He opened it up, found the blade that doubled as a bottle opener, took the cap off his soda, and passed the knife around the table. Bruno reached a paw through the bars of his cage, trying to get at either Thaddeus or the soft drinks, and Thaddeus moved his chair a bit farther away.

"First things first: did you speak to Ahasuerus or any of the others on your way to the bus?"

"You told me not to," replied Mr. Romany.

"Good," said Thaddeus, allowing himself the luxury of a little smile. "I admire a man who does what he's told. It seems to me that I also told you to see if you could come up with a mutually agreeable proposition."

Mr. Romany nodded. "We both know that you've got me over a barrel," he said, "so I'm going to give you my best offer, and I think it will meet with your approval."

121

"*Our* approval," said Thaddeus. "Tojo's also my business adviser."

"Oh. I didn't know," said Mr. Romany, looking a bit flustered.

"Now you do. Please continue."

"Mr. Flint, I've got to have Ahasuerus and his group back. That much is nonnegotiable."

"Don't use words like 'nonnegotiable' so early in the conversation," said Thaddeus. "I find them irritating."

"Nevertheless, I absolutely must have them back. My career depends on it. My proposal is simply this: if you'll return them, I will convince my superiors to use your carnival and your carnival alone as the base for all future excursion groups."

"Can you do that?"

"I think so."

"You *think* so?" repeated Thaddeus, arching his eyebrows.

"Let me rephrase that," said Mr. Romany. "I know that I can."

"What if one of your superiors decides he doesn't like the idea?"

"They're half a galaxy away. They'll be guided by my recommendations."

"And after Ahasuerus tells them what happened here?"

"It will be his word against mine. And yours."

"His word and that of eleven other aliens," corrected Thaddeus.

"Mr. Flint, I don't mean to speak down to you, but you simply have no idea how big the galaxy actually *is*. It would take my employer's bureaucracy years, lifetimes, to round up the necessary testimony and evidence."

"And what do you get out of this?" asked Thaddeus.

"My job."

"And what else?"

"One-third."

"One-third of what?"

"Everything. It will be worth it, Mr. Flint. Look how much having Ahasuerus' group has already improved your business. And besides, it won't last forever. I'll be off this dirtball in three or four years."

"Yeah? Where will you go?"

"I have three more planets to open up while I'm in this shape."

"What do you mean—*this* shape?"

"This," he said, indicating himself, "is not my real body.'

"You can change your shape?" asked Thaddeus, suddenly alert.

"Not at will," said Mr. Romany with a small laugh. "I've been surgically altered."

"You have?"

"Yes. It's a relatively simple process. It takes about two to three weeks."

"But why did you do it?"

"I'm an advance man, Mr. Flint. I make the initial contacts on planets that have not yet joined our community of worlds, and of course it behooves me to meet the natives not only on their own turf, so to speak, but in their own image as well."

"And there are three other worlds populated by men?" asked Thaddeus.

"Not exactly. I'm not totally like you, Mr. Flint. My coloration is a little different, my eyes are more widely set, my fingernails are false, and I have a rudimentary tail. But I'm close enough to pass as one of you, just as—depending on which features I emphasize—I'll be close enough to pass as an inhabitant of each of the other three worlds on my current agenda. Altering to accommodate three or four worlds at once saves considerable time, expense, and personal discomfort."

"Does everyone in your organization alter his shape?"

"Oh, no. Very few of us do, in fact. But it does help to advance one's career."

"I see," said Thaddeus. "And you plan to be on some other world in a few years?"

Mr. Romany nodded. "Five years at the most," he said. "Do we have an agreement?"

"No," said Thaddeus.

"No?" repeated Mr. Romany in astonishment. "But why not?"

"First of all, I find it highly unlikely that all future aliens will be as docile as this group. Second, I'm having enough trouble keeping this bunch alive, and I have no assurances that you won't foist a batch of even sicklier

123

ones off on me. Third, I'm already making a bundle without cutting you in for one-third. And fourth, you overestimate your importance. Your word will never hold up against Ahasuerus'."

"What makes you think not?"

"Because if *I* can see through you in ten minutes, so can whoever has to decide the case. You're a two-bit clerk who's fighting for his job. He's an honorable man with nothing to hide. Who do you think they'll believe?"

"What do *you* know about honorable men?" said Mr. Romany hotly.

"I don't have to be a horse to know that Secretariat was a good one," replied Thaddeus.

"You won't agree to it?" repeated Mr. Romany desperately.

"Of course not. But I figured you'd come up with some cockamamie scheme like this, so I've prepared a little counteroffer. Would you like to hear it?"

"Go ahead."

"Okay," said Thaddeus. "Quit the company and come to work for me. Keep the aliens healthy and happy and I'll give you five percent of the take."

"Quit the company?"

"Beats getting fired, doesn't it?" said Thaddeus with a smile.

"But I'd have to stay in this shape, on this world," protested Mr. Romany.

"It could be worse. You could be in Tojo's shape," commented Thaddeus.

The lion roared just then, and Mr. Romany jumped. It took both of them a minute or two to calm down.

"I don't think I can do it," said Mr. Romany. "Stay here forever?"

"It might not be forever," said Thaddeus. "I might get tired of it."

"You? Tired of money?"

"You never can tell," said Thaddeus.

"I'll have to think about it," said Mr. Romany.

"Take your time."

"That's the one commodity I don't have in abundance."

"I know," said Thaddeus. "How long before your mother ship sends out a distress signal?"

"What do you know about a mother ship?" said Mr. Romany sharply.

"I know twelve aliens didn't cross the galaxy in a little shuttlecraft. It stands to reason there are other groups on Earth, and that you've got a big ship in orbit. Of course, you're welcome to deny it, if it'll make you feel any better."

"It's up there," admitted Mr. Romany.

"And of course it's too big to land."

Mr. Romany nodded. "If Ahasuerus isn't back aboard it in four more days, they'll call my superiors for instructions."

"I thought he was over his time limit already."

"The excursion was to be for fourteen days, but the situation is not considered critical until twenty days have passed."

"Well, you seem to have a problem on your hands, Mr. Romany," said Thaddeus. "Why not go home and think it over for another day?"

"Fifteen percent," said Mr. Romany suddenly.

Thaddeus laughed. "Get out of here, you fucking amateur!"

Mr. Romany left, and Thaddeus walked to the refrigerator again, pulled out a couple of slices of Swiss cheese, and tossed them to the leopards, who ignored them.

"Oh, well," he shrugged. "You can't please everyone."

"Thaddeus," I said, "what's going to happen?"

"Who knows?" he replied. "But it sure as hell is gonna be interesting, isn't it?"

13.

It started snowing very heavily about an hour after Mr. Romany left. Thaddeus turned on the radio, found out that there were traveler's advisory warnings out and that many of the roads had been closed, and decided to shut down the carnival for the day. He sent Big Alvin and me around to post signs to that effect. It took us about twenty minutes, and when we were done we hurried back to the dormitory tent to warm up and have some of Queenie's coffee.

Thaddeus was sitting at a table with Mr. Ahasuerus, the astronomy book turned open to a photo of the Crab Nebula, listening intently to the blue man.

"*This* I recognize," Mr. Ahasuerus was saying, pointing to the photo. "But you must understand that your stellar configurations are completely different from those I am used to. In other words, I may be acquainted with many of these stars, but not in the positions where they appear to you."

Thaddeus pushed the book over to him. "Is there anything else you recognize?"

The blue man thumbed through the rest of the pages, staring at each one carefully. Finally he shook his head. "I am neither an astronomer nor a navigator," he said. "This one," he added, pointing toward a tiny spot on a huge picture, "could be Mr. Romany's home star. It's the right color, and it seems to be in the right star cluster. But of course I can't be sure."

"How did your company ever pick a loser like Romany in the first place?"

Mr. Ahasuerus shrugged. "We employ hundreds of thousands of beings. From what I know of him, his record has been exemplary."

"Yeah. Well, beware of Greeks bearing gifts and hot-shot junior executives with exemplary records." Thaddeus

126

paused for a minute to light a cigarette. "Tell me a little bit about your organization."

"We're a loosely knit community of worlds that have united for economic and cultural benefits," replied Mr. Ahasuerus. "We bear absolutely no resemblance to the quasi-military empires that your more imaginative entertainments envision."

"That's not what I meant. Tell me about the company you work for."

"What do you wish to know?"

"Who runs it? How big is it? What does it do?" He exhaled a stream of smoke and smiled. "I feel more at home talking about businesses than galactic civilizations."

"So do I," admitted Mr. Ahasuerus, flashing his teeth in what I supposed was his equivalent of a grin. "We are what you would call a conglomerate. We have branches on hundreds of worlds, and we deal in everything from manufacturing to real estate to space travel."

"How did you come to pose as a sideshow?"

"I told you. We attract less—"

"I know that," interrupted Thaddeus. "But that means you must have sideshows on your home planet."

"No," corrected the blue man, "but they are quite common on many of our community of worlds. Indeed, had they not been known to Earth, I am sure Mr. Romany would have recommended that we bypass the planet. After all, there are thousands of other worlds worthy of interest."

"Romany told me he was surgically altered."

"That's true. It is a complex and painful operation, though relatively brief."

"What did he look like originally?" asked Thaddeus.

"I have no idea."

"How did they know to make him look the way he does?"

"We tend not to visit worlds that do not transmit television signals," said Mr. Ahasuerus. "Does that answer your question?"

"I suppose so," replied Thaddeus. "What kind of currency do you use?"

"It varies from world to world."

"Doesn't that get pretty complicated after a while?"

"It is no more complicated within the community than

127

dealing in dollars and pounds and yen is to the nations of your world. Of course, when we travel beyond the community, a certain amount of creative financing is required."

"What particular kind of creative financing did Romany indulge in to bankroll your carnival?" asked Thaddeus.

"I really couldn't say," answered the blue man.

"I'm beginning to get the impression that you could teach us one hell of a lot about bureaucracies." He turned to me. "Wouldn't the Rigger make one hell of an advance man?" he said with an amused laugh. "You could plunk him down penniless on any world in the galaxy with nothing but a deck of cards and a pair of dice, and he'd own half the planet by nightfall."

He pulled a flask out of his pocket and took a long swallow. A gust of wind whipped through the canvas a minute later, and I asked if I could have a sip. He shrugged and handed it to me, and I took a small mouthful. It burned my lips, and stayed hot all the way down.

"What was it?" I gasped.

"What do you care? It'll keep you warm." He took the flask back and then, as an afterthought, offered it to Mr. Ahasuerus.

"No, thank you," said the blue man.

"Right," said Thaddeus. "It would probably kill you." He screwed the top on and put it back in his pocket. "What are the winters like where you come from? Do they ever get this cold?"

"From time to time," said Mr. Ahasuerus. "Though it has been many years since I was on my home planet."

"Don't you ever miss it?" I asked.

"Not with so many new worlds to see," he said. "Our friend the Rubber Man would have you believe that one world is pretty much like another, but he's wrong: each is unique and individual, and each is fascinating in its own way."

"Even this one?" asked Thaddeus.

"Of course," said the blue man.

"How long have you been on the road, so to speak?"

"Oh, perhaps twenty of your years."

"And you have no desire to return home?"

"I've *seen* home, Mr. Flint," said Mr. Ahasuerus.

"These others"—he indicated the rest of the aliens—"are merely tourists and vacationers. I am a wanderer."

"You *were* a wanderer," Thaddeus corrected him.

"I will be again. Whatever agreement you make or do not make with Mr. Romany, you won't kill us."

"You're sure about that, are you?" asked Thaddeus.

"Yes," said the blue man. "First of all, it is in your best interest to keep us alive and working. And second," he added, looking straight into Thaddeus' eyes, "you're an exploiter, not a killer."

"You think not?"

"I think not."

Thaddeus shook his head. "I give a rubdown to the rainbow man and try to keep Dapper Dan alive, and all of a sudden you seem to think you're dealing with some kind of a pushover. Maybe I've been taking it a little too easy on you."

"What purpose would be served by abusing us?" asked Mr. Ahasuerus.

"Maybe it would make me feel better," said Thaddeus.

Mr. Ahasuerus was about to reply when Big Alvin walked up to the table.

"Yeah?" said Thaddeus.

"Four-Eyes is out of iron pills," said the big guy.

"You're just noticing that now?" said Thaddeus. "It's a damned good thing he's not depending on *you* to keep track of that stuff."

"Then you've got some more?"

"I sent Monk out for them when I closed the show," said Thaddeus. Alvin went back to his post, and Thaddeus turned to me with an amused smile on his face. "When I heard the roads were closed I figured that Four-Eyes was in for a bad night. Then I remembered all of Monk's stories about how he used to go hunting in the Klondike, so I went over to his bus and offered him fifty bucks to walk into town and pick up the pills. He finally agreed to go when I got up to eighty dollars, and just when I was sure that I was sending the poor son of a bitch out to freeze, he locked the money in that little metal coinbox he keeps in the bear cage, walked to his closet, and pulled out a pair of snowshoes and a fur coat that must have been made of forty sealskins. He's so goddam warm that when he gets back I think the first thing he's going to ask for is a cold beer."

"When is he due?" I asked.

"Another hour or two. It depends on the snow." His gaze fell on the Cyclops. "Look at him!" he said disgustedly. "Healthy as a horse."

"Should I check on Dapper Dan and Rainbow again?" I asked.

"No. Swede's with 'em. They'll be okay." He looked out at the blizzard. "I'll tell you what you *can* do, though. Take turns with Alvin making the rounds every hour or so to make sure there aren't any locals freezing to death out there. If you find any, take 'em over to the Hothouse until they can figure out how to get home—and if they've got any money, send the Rigger by to pay them a friendly little visit." He looked up and saw Scratch approaching us hesitantly. "Well, well, what have we here?"

"Mr. Flint," said the Horned Demon.

"Yeah? What do you want?"

"The Man of Many Colors is an especially close friend of mine. I wonder if you could tell me how his condition is progressing."

"Pretty much the same," said Thaddeus. "Maybe a little better. It's hard to tell."

Scratch shifted his weight uneasily. "I would like your permission to visit him."

"Out of the question," said Thaddeus. "None of you leaves the tent."

"I know that you are short-handed because of us," persisted Scratch. "Since we will not be on display tonight, I would be happy to take the place of whoever is tending to him and to the Missing Link."

"I'm sure you would," said Thaddeus. "I'm sure you would be equally happy to hit the Midway running and never look back."

"How far could I get in this weather?" said Scratch with a smile. "Where would I go?"

"A rule is a rule," said Thaddeus. "Forget it."

"It would mean a lot to him," continued Scratch.

"You don't listen too good, do you?" said Thaddeus irritably.

"Neither do you," said Scratch, obviously nervous but obstinately holding his ground. "I told you that I will not

130

try to escape. I simply want to bring comfort to my friend."

"Swede *has* been over there an awfully long time, Thaddeus," I said.

"You, too?" he said, turning to me.

"What harm could it do, Thaddeus?" I said. "Nobody's going to run away on a day like this."

"Shut up, both of you!" he yelled.

I jumped back, because that tone of voice usually preceded a blow, but he just sat motionless at the table, staring at his coffee cup, while Scratch walked unhappily back to his cot.

Finally, after almost half an hour had passed, Thaddeus got up, looked out the door at the snow, and walked back to me.

"All right, you fucking dwarf," he said with a sigh. "We'll do it your way. Hunt up a coat for Scratch and take him over to the trailer, and tell Swede to come over here to grab some dinner. And when you're done with that, tell the Dancer to bunk with Diggs or Monk tonight. I want his trailer."

"What for?"

"Because I'm getting goddamned sick and tired of sharing mine with a couple of aliens," he said.

I took the Horned Demon to our trailer, spent about five minutes convincing Swede that Thaddeus had really agreed to it, and then went off to find the Dancer. I finally found him sitting in the makeshift grandstand of the specialty tent, staring blindly into the past. I don't think he even knew it was snowing.

He agreed to move in with Monk for the night, and I went back to the dormitory tent to tell Thaddeus that the arrangements had been made.

While I was gone he had finished his entire flask of whiskey, and he was a little unsteady on his feet when he stood up. I helped him to the door, and then led the way to the Dancer's trailer.

It was freezing when we entered it—the Dancer had forgotten to turn the heat on—and I spent the next couple of minutes making it liveable, while Thaddeus rooted through the kitchen cabinets until he came up with a bottle of Scotch, a present from some infatuated teen-aged fan of the Dancer's.

The trailer looked more than neat and well-kept: it

131

looked unused. The bed was wrinkled, but I doubted that the Dancer had crawled under the covers since he'd owned it. There were no crumbs in the kitchen or on the breakfast table, but again I felt that was due to his lifestyle—if that is the word for it—rather than any fetish for cleaning up after himself. There were photographs and tintypes of all the famous outlaws and lawmen of the Old West hanging on the walls, and I had a feeling that all of Billybuck's time in the trailer was spent sitting in his big leather chair staring at them, or dozing on top of his covers. Walking through the trailer produced an eerie feeling—but then, all carny people are strange. The Dancer was just a little stranger than most.

Thaddeus had finished almost half the bottle by the time I returned to him, and I cautioned him to slow down a little.

"Why?" he said. "The sooner I get good and drunk, the sooner I'll forget about those goddamned freaks."

"They're aliens, Thaddeus."

"Aliens, freaks, what the hell's the difference?" He stared moodily at a photograph of the O.K. Corral. "I'm losing control," he muttered at last.

"I don't understand what you mean."

"Haven't you got eyes? Don't you see what's going on?" He looked over at me with an odd expression on his face. I wrote it off to the liquor.

"You're not making any sense, Thaddeus."

"Goddammit, Tojo! Ahasuerus acts more like my father than my prisoner. And that blasted Horned Demon knows that no one can leave the tent, and even so he thought he could get away with it."

"He *did* get away with it," I pointed out.

"That's what I mean! Why should I give a flying fuck about whether the rainbow man is happy or not?" He pounded a fist down on the arm of his chair. "Look at me! I'm sitting here staring at pictures of Wyatt Earp and Jesse James. And why? Because my own trailer has been turned into a nursing home for sick aliens!"

"It was your idea," I said.

"I know!" he yelled. "But why the hell did I think of it, Tojo? I don't *do* things like that!"

I didn't know what to say, so I simply kept quiet and stared at him as he took another drink.

"I'm losing control of things!" he repeated. "And that goddamned blue man knows it. He just sits there, taking everything I can dish out and thanking me for it. Why doesn't he fight back?"

"I don't know, Thaddeus." I reached out for the Scotch. "You'd better take it a little easy with this stuff."

"Get your hands off it!" he said hotly, grabbing the bottle back and taking another long swallow. "You're on *their* side, aren't you?"

"I'm on *my* side," I said noncommittally.

"Don't lie to me, you little dwarf! Everyone's on their side—you, Alma, Queenie, Monk, even the Dancer if he's spent two seconds thinking about it. The only one who doesn't give a damn about them is Romany."

"And you," I said.

"Right," he said without conviction. "And me."

He looked at the bottle for a minute, then hurled it against the wall, where it exploded into a thousand tiny fragments.

Then he stood up and walked groggily into the bedroom. I heard the springs squeak as he flopped down on the bed, I heard his shoes hit the floor as he kicked them off, and then I heard him mutter, in an unhappy and bewildered voice:

"What *is* happening to me?"

14.

I woke up to the sound of Thaddeus' voice.

At first I thought I had fallen asleep in the Dancer's trailer, but as my mind became clearer I remembered trudging back to my own bed. Wondering if one of the aliens had become sicker, I threw on a robe and walked out to the living room.

Scratch was still there, and Rainbow—now a much richer shade of blue, with ripples of red running up and down his torso—was sitting on a chair, obviously much improved. Thaddeus was leaning back on the couch, his feet propped up on the beat-up coffee table.

The sun, beating in through the windows, made my eyes water, and I realized that it was midmorning.

"Where's Dapper Dan?" I asked.

Thaddeus smiled. "Even potential suicides have to use the facilities every now and then."

"Aren't you afraid he might climb out the window?"

Thaddeus shook his head. "Not with eight inches of snow on the ground. He may be mixed up, but he's not crazy. It takes a long time to freeze to death, and it's been my observation that people who try to overdose usually have an aversion to painful and extended death scenes." He looked up as the Missing Link entered the room. "What did I tell you?"

"May I pass?" said Dapper Dan patiently.

"Be my guest," said Thaddeus, swinging his feet off the table to provide the Missing Link with a path to the one empty chair in the room.

"What are you doing here?" I asked Thaddeus.

"I live here," he said. "Also, I woke up with a hangover you wouldn't believe, and our Billybuck's long and strong suit isn't hangover remedies, so I figured I might as well bite the bullet and sober up the hard way. I thought I'd die before I got halfway here, but by the time I reached the door I was feeling mildly human again.

Which, considering our present company, isn't all that bad a thing to be."

"You're looking better, Rainbow," I said.

"I am recovering," he answered. Then he turned to Thaddeus. "If you need me, I can probably be put back on display this afternoon."

"Forget it," said Thaddeus. "You'd turn into an icicle before I got you over to the tent. You'll stay here for another day or two. You, too," he added to Dapper Dan. "That is, if you want to."

"It makes no difference," said the Missing Link.

"Jesus, you'd depress a hyena," said Thaddeus. "Relax. I'm going to be talking deal to Romany again today."

"Nothing will come of it," said Dapper Dan morosely.

"Nothing like a little optimism to start the day," said Thaddeus. "I don't suppose you've ever considered becoming a comedian?"

"We don't have any on my world."

"Somehow I'm not surprised," said Thaddeus dryly. He stood up and walked to the door. "I'm going to check on the others. Come on over after you get dressed, Tojo."

"What about me?" asked Scratch.

"Don't drink all my beer," said Thaddeus, going out the door.

"Thank you!" Scratch shouted after him, but the door was already closed and I don't think he heard it.

I spent the next few minutes shaving and getting dressed. Then I made my bed, and since Rainbow looked as if he was up for the day, I made his as well. Finally I put my coat and gloves on and walked out into the cold, closing the door as quickly as possible so as not to subject Rainbow to a draft.

The snow had stopped falling sometime during the night, snowplows were clearing the roads, the sun was finally shining, and those few birds that hadn't yet flown south were scouring the grounds in search of food.

Thaddeus had left a trail of deep footprints in the snow, leading directly to the dormitory tent. As I followed them I saw Gloria heading over to the girlie show to start her morning exercises, and we waved to each other. The only other person up and around was the Rigger, who looked for all the world like a poker game in search of a place to happen. He hollered over to me that he was going to the Hothouse in a few minutes and that if any marks showed up early I should send them over, as he would be only too happy to entertain them.

Thaddeus and Mr. Ahasuerus were sitting together at a table when I got to the dormitory tent. The blue man looked up and gave me his somewhat frightening equivalent of a smile of greeting, and Thaddeus gestured me to pull up a chair and join them, which I did after first getting a cup of coffee from Queenie.

"So they really don't have any?" Thaddeus was saying with a look of total disbelief on his face.

Mr. Ahasuerus shook his head. "It seems to be an art form—if that is the proper word for it—that is confined solely to your planet."

"That's hard to believe."

"What are you talking about?" I asked.

"Mr. Ahasuerus has just informed me that we have the only strippers in the whole damned galaxy," said Thaddeus. "Considering how many races seem to be running around your community of worlds, it just seems kind of farfetched to me that they could all be so uninterested in sex."

"You are confusing sex with titillation," replied the blue man. "Many of the races don't even wear clothing."

"That's funny," remarked Thaddeus. "I would have thought all civilized races wore clothes."

"Most sentient races can control their environments. Those who retain the desire for clothing do so from reasons totally extraneous to protection from the elements: shame, morality, fashion."

"How about lion tamers?" asked Thaddeus.

"Most of our circuses and carnivals have animal trainers," replied Mr. Ahasuerus. "Some of them work with animals that are of a magnitude that would make your friend Monk think twice about entering a cage with them."

"And trick-shot artists?"

"A few," said the blue man. "But, to be honest, none of them with the skill of Billybuck Dancer. I have often wondered how and where he acquired it."

"You and me both," said Thaddeus.

Alvin walked in just then, carrying all our CLOSED signs.

136

"What do you think *you're* doing?" demanded Thaddeus.

"The roads are open," replied Big Alvin.

"I didn't tell you to take those down."

"But——"

"Put 'em back up. We're moving out."

"Where are we going?" I asked.

"I don't know yet. But the weather's too lousy to stay up here any longer."

Alvin shrugged and went back out to post the signs again.

"Mr. Flint," said Mr. Ahasuerus. "I feel I must interject a word at this point."

"Save your breath," said Thaddeus. "I know what you're going to say."

"Do you?"

"You're going to tell me that if you don't report to your mother ship in the next seventy-two hours all hell is going to break loose."

"How did you know that?" asked Mr. Ahasuerus, genuinely surprised.

"Your friend Romany's got a big mouth."

"Indeed he does," agreed Mr. Ahasuerus. "That does not, however, negate the truth of what he said."

"I know," said Thaddeus.

"What do you propose to do about it?"

"I've been giving the matter a lot of thought. I'll let you know." He fumbled through his pockets for a cigarette, pulled it out, and lit it. "By the way, Rainbow's up and around."

"I'm gratified to hear it."

"And I don't think you have to worry about Dapper Dan killing himself. He's just spent a couple of days thinking about what almost happened to his immortal if somewhat displaced soul."

"Good."

"It occurs to me," remarked Thaddeus, "that you must have one hell of a time nursemaiding your tourists around the galaxy."

"Most of them are not hardened travelers," agreed Mr. Ahasuerus wryly. "Still, it has been a fulfilling job in many ways."

"How did you come by it?"

"I beg your pardon?"

"Your job," said Thaddeus. "What made you choose it?"

"I was selected."

"Yeah? What were your qualifications—languages and things like that?"

"That, too," said Mr. Ahasuerus. "When is Mr. Romany due to return?"

Thaddeus shrugged. "Who knows? Sometime today."

"What has he offered you already?" asked the blue man.

"Nothing that interests me," replied Thaddeus. He turned to me. "Tojo, as long as you're just sitting there like a rock, why don't you pass the word that we're breaking down the show and packing it onto the trucks?"

I put my coat back on and went around the grounds, telling Diggs and Monk and anyone else I could find to start taking the carnival apart. Most of them wanted to know where we were going, but even though I couldn't tell them they were all pretty happy with the decision. In their eyes, *anywhere* was better than Vermont in the snow. (Monk did tell me, though, that if Thaddeus went back up to Maine, he was taking his animals and going to Florida with them.)

Thaddeus and Mr. Ahasuerus were still sitting at the table when I got back.

"You didn't see our friend Romany out there, did you?" asked Thaddeus.

"No," I replied.

"Poor bastard is probably reading the Help Wanted ads," said Thaddeus with a chuckle.

"Have you decided what you're going to say to him?" asked Mr. Ahasuerus.

"Pretty much," he said. "Of course, he's got to show up first. Right about now he's probably sitting in his room wondering how he can bribe or blackmail me."

"Do you really think so?' asked the blue man curiously.

"I can read that son of a bitch like a book," smiled Thaddeus. "*You're* the only one I have problems with."

"Me?" asked Mr. Ahasuerus.

"Don't look so damned innocent. The others all make sense. You don't."

138

"In what way?"

"Romany's just a guy who's fighting tooth and nail to hang onto his job. Dapper Dan's a very confused religious freak. The Lizard would stick a knife in my ribs if I ever turned my back on him. The same with the Sphinx. The rest of them are just chattel, a bunch of tourists out for a holiday. But *you*—you ought to be ready to kill me, or be so damned scared of me you don't know which way is up."

"And you find that unusual?" asked Mr. Ahasuerus.

"It's been my experience that the whole damned universe can be divided into meat and meat-eaters. You fall somewhere in between."

"And this disturbs you?"

"It did," admitted Thaddeus. "Now it just puzzles me."

"You asked me a few minutes ago why I was chosen for this position," said the blue man. He placed a finger on his face. "*This* is the reason."

"I'm not sure that I understand you," said Thaddeus.

"To borrow from your religious teachings, I have two cheeks. The assumption is that if I turn the other one often enough, sooner or later a sentient being will get tired of hitting it and will find some more constructive means of communication."

Thaddeus stared at him for a very long time. "You're a very unusual man, Mr. Ahasuerus," he said at last.

"Thank you."

"Put the two of us together and you might come up with a normal human being."

"You might indeed," said the blue man.

"Or at least an interesting one." Thaddeus stared at him again, seemingly lost in thought. Finally he turned to me. "Tojo, tell the Dancer I need his trailer again."

"When?" I asked.

"Right now."

I walked to the door.

"And bring a coat back for Mr. Ahasuerus," he called after me.

I found the Dancer in the Hothouse. He offered no objection to letting Thaddeus use his trailer, and even loaned me his fur-lined jacket to take back to Mr. Ahasuerus. When I returned to the tent, Thaddeus was on

139

his feet. He took the coat from me and handed it to the blue man.

"We're going over there to talk a little business," he said. "I don't want to be disturbed."

"What if Mr. Romany shows up?" I asked.

"I almost forgot about him. All right—when he gets here have him wait in the Hothouse. Then come over and let me know he's on the grounds."

Then Thaddeus and Mr. Ahasuerus walked out the door and went over to the Dancer's trailer.

"What the hell is going on?" asked Queenie, staring after them.

"I'm not sure," I told her.

I tried to keep busy around the tent, sweeping the floors and checking on Snoopy and Pumpkin every few minutes. I asked Alvin for the time twice, and when an hour had passed I got so curious that I couldn't keep my mind on my work any longer, so I sat down and thumbed through Thaddeus' astronomy book and wondered what was happening inside the Dancer's trailer.

Mr. Romany arrived half an hour later, looking very nervous and fidgety. I ushered him over to the Hothouse, then went to the trailer and knocked on the door.

Thaddeus stuck his head out a minute later. "Yeah?"

"Mr. Romany is here."

"Tell him to wait."

The door slammed shut, and I returned to the Hothouse to tell Mr. Romany that Thaddeus wasn't ready to see him yet. The Rigger walked up and offered to take his mind off the waiting with a friendly little game of gin rummy, but Mr. Romany just shook his head and kept drumming his fingers against a support post.

Finally, after another hour had passed, Thaddeus opened the door again and called for me.

"Yes?" I said, walking about halfway to the trailer.

"Send him over now. Then I want you to go to my van and bring me the map I keep in my glove compartment."

"You keep a lot of maps there," I said. "Which one do you want?"

He laughed. "Bring 'em all, you nosy little bastard."

I escorted Mr. Romany to the trailer, hunted up the maps and returned with them, and then walked over to the dormitory tent. Every now and then I would step outside to see if the meeting had broken up yet, but as night fell over the snow-covered Vermont countryside none of the three had emerged from the Dancer's trailer.

15.

The meeting lasted until almost ten o'clock. Then the three of them—Thaddeus, Mr. Ahasuerus, and Mr. Romany—got into Thaddeus' van and drove off without a word to anyone.

I went to bed around midnight, and slept very restlessly, which was unusual for me. I woke up at seven, checked the clock by my bed, and went back to sleep for another two hours. Dapper Dan, Rainbow, and Scratch were up and moving around by the time I got my clothes on, and Scratch offered me a cup of hot tea, apologizing for the lack of coffee but explaining that while he could speak the language fluently he still had some difficulties reading it, and that the instructions on the electric coffee maker had been a little beyond him.

I thanked him, took the tea, and walked over to the couch, where I sat down and stared out the window. The van still wasn't back, and I began wondering if it had skidded off some ice-covered Vermont road.

I wasted an hour sitting around the trailer and loafing, and had just decided to go over to the dormitory tent when the big blue-and-white Dodge maxivan pulled up and Thaddeus emerged from it. For a moment I thought he was alone, but then Mr. Ahasuerus and Mr. Romany got out, and all three climbed the four stairs to the trailer door.

"Jesus, it's cold out there!" said Thaddeus, ushering the other two inside and rubbing his hands together briskly.

"Good morning," said Scratch.

"Good morning yourself," said Thaddeus. "Tojo, are we set to roll?"

"Everything's loaded except the dormitory tent," I told him.

"Good. Have Monk back his bus up to it and load the aliens into the back. Then have him stop by here to pick up Scratch, Rainbow, and Dapper Dan." He turned to Mr. Ahasuerus and Mr. Romany. "You two want to ride with the others?"

"That will be perfectly acceptable," said the blue man.

"Where are we going?" I asked.

"Not too far away," said Thaddeus. "Tell everyone to form a caravan and follow me."

"Who did *I* go with?"

"You go with me. And bring along a pencil and some paper."

Monk got the aliens loaded in about an hour—we took a little more care with them this time—and then, when all the trucks and vans and trailers and buses were lined up, I climbed into the van and Thaddeus pulled out and turned south on a nearby state highway.

"Got that paper?" he asked, lighting up a cigarette.

"Yes," I said, pulling out a notepad and a ballpoint pen.

"Good. Write these names down: Monk, the Dancer, Diggs." Suddenly the car ahead of us hit a patch of ice and started skidding, and Thaddeus concentrated on his driving for the next mile or so. "Where the hell was I?" he asked at last.

"Monk, Dancer, Diggs."

"Right. Put down Gloria's name, too." He paused for a minute. "Barbara and Priscilla. And Swede. And what's the name of that blond girl who works the Fascination game for the Rigger—the one with the big boobs?"

"Jenny."

"Right. Jenny. Put her name down. And Stogie, I suppose." He paused again, as if considering. "Yeah. Put Stogie's name down. And that redhead with the tight little ass who worked with the Dancer last month before we stuck her out with Diggs."

"Lori?"

"Yeah, I think so." He snuffed out his cigarette. "And Fast Johnny."

Fast Johnny Carp was the Rigger's second-in-command, and I scribbled his name on the pad.

"You got it all written down?" he asked.

"Yes."

"Okay. Fold it up, stick it in your pocket, and don't lose it."

Thaddeus turned the radio on then, cursed it roundly when he couldn't find any sports events, and finally settled for a rather tinny country-and-western music station. We drove in silence for almost two hours, then turned off onto a side road, went about a quarter of a mile, and came to a stop.

Thaddeus reached over to the glove compartment, opened it, and pulled out a couple of sheets of paper that bore his unmistakable scrawl. He studied them for a moment, then laid them on the dashboard and started the van again.

The terrain became hilly, then mountainous, and the road grew more hazardous. Thaddeus kept referring to his notes, though, and continued driving despite the dangerous conditions. At last he came to a large flat field and pulled onto it, and the rest of the caravan followed suit.

"Okay," he said, turning off the ignition. "Round up everyone but the aliens and tell them to come on over here. I've got something to say to them."

It took a few minutes—there were thirty-two of us—but before long we were all standing in front of the van. Then Thaddeus climbed out and faced us.

"I just want to announce that there are going to be a few changes around here," he said, walking back and forth to keep warm. "I've taken on a couple of partners, and from now on we're going to have two divisions, just like the Greatest Show on Earth."

He paused for a reaction, but it was too cold for anyone to do anything except just listen.

"Most of you will be staying with the main division, the one you've been working with. Mr. Romany will be in charge of it. You'll play up and down the Atlantic seaboard, just like we've always done. Everyone who stays with this division will be getting raises, starting today."

That brought a rousing, though brief, cheer.

"Mr. Ahasuerus and I will be taking the other division a little farther afield," he continued. "It's too damned cold to tell you what we have in mind while we're out here, but Tojo will hunt each of you up and we'll talk about it in my trailer. That's all."

He walked around to the trailer, which had been hitched to the back of the van, and climbed into it. Everyone else dispersed to go to the warmth of their vehicles, but I managed to grab Monk before he could return to the bus and told him that Thaddeus wanted to speak to him.

"Probably wants to tell me why I shouldn't expect a raise," he grumbled, walking over to the trailer.

He emerged half an hour later with the strangest expression on his face, and I sent the Dancer in.

"That's the damnedest thing I ever heard!" Monk exclaimed. "I still don't think I believe him!"

"What did he say?" I asked.

"Let's go over to Buffalo Bill's trailer," he said. "It's too cold to stand out here talking."

I followed him, and by the time we got there the Dancer was already on his way back. Diggs was puttering around his Winnebago, and I yelled over to him that it was his turn to speak to Thaddeus.

"Did he tell *you* what he told me?" asked Monk when we were inside and the Dancer was shutting the door behind us.

"Probably," said the Dancer.

"Then what are you doing back so soon? Didn't you have any questions?"

"Nope."

"He tells you that you're going to a bunch of god-damned worlds nobody has ever heard of and you ain't got any questions?"

"I don't care who watches me, as long as I get to do my act," said the Dancer with a shrug.

"That's not what I mean!" said Monk in exasperation. "Do you really buy all this shit about the freaks coming from other worlds?"

"Who cares where they come from?" asked the Dancer gently.

"Don't you understand what I'm saying to you?" insisted Monk.

"Sure. It's just not very important. Are you going or staying?"

"I'll give you a hundred-to-one it's a bunch of bull-shit!" said Monk. Then he flashed a guilty little smile. "But just in case it ain't, wild horses couldn't keep me off that ship." He turned to me. "What do you know about all this, Tojo?"

"They're aliens," I said.

"Who's going along? Thaddeus said it would only be people he needed. Of course," he added with a wink, "I'll bet another hundred-to-one that he suddenly finds one hell of a need for Jenny."

"He'll be talking to Diggs and Gloria and some of the others," I said unhappily.

"Good!" said Monk. "I can't imagine going on the road without the Rigger, no matter *how* far away the road is."

And I couldn't imagine why Stogie was on the list and I wasn't. Of course, he'd work in the strip show, and I wasn't much good at anything except tending to a batch of sick tourists who were probably going straight home, but still . . .

"How about Alma?" asked Monk.

"I don't think so," I replied.

"That's one way to get rid of 'em once you're tired of 'em!" laughed Monk. "And I'll bet you he's not taking Big Alvin either."

"He's not on the list," I said.

"Gloria's going to need another protector," said Monk. "I think I'll give the job to Bruno."

There was a knock at the door, and a few seconds later Diggs came in. He threw his coat on a chair and walked over to join us.

"Gloria's in there now," he told me, "and Thaddeus says he wants to see Swede next."

"Swede?" said Monk. "What the hell do we need *him* for?"

"You sound like you *believe* all this shit," said Diggs.

"It's a bunch of bullshit," said Monk. "But it *is* a fascinating idea, isn't it?"

"I'd have to learn a whole new batch of card games," said the Rigger.

"Well, if you think you're too old . . ." began Monk, an amused expression on his face.

"You sound just like Thaddeus!" snapped the Rigger.

"What do you mean?"

"He got me so mad I said I'd go just to show him that there isn't anyone anywhere that can con a mark like Jason Diggs." He shrugged. "So I guess I'm going," he concluded wryly.

The next few minutes were devoted to the future, as

146

Monk and Diggs started laying bets on what kind of life forms they'd run into, and I started considering what I was going to do with my life, now that my family was leaving. It wasn't much of a family, it was filled with frauds and misfits and grotesques, but it was the only family I had, and suddenly I began to feel very empty inside. Memories of my childhood and my classmates and the sanitarium began racing through my mind, and I felt like I was going to cry, so I put on my coat and quietly walked out the door where no one could see me.

Gloria was just coming out of Thaddeus' trailer, and I tracked down Swede and sent him over. Then I noticed that someone had set up the Hothouse, and I stopped by to warm up. Alma was sitting there, all alone, huddled up in her overcoat.

"Hi," I said.

"What's happening, Tojo?" she said. "Why is he talking to Gloria?"

"He wants her for the new division."

"Someone told me you have the list. Am I on it?"

"No, Alma," I said. "You're not."

"And Queenie?"

"No."

"I thought for a minute he was going to try to split us up." She paused. "Where is this new division going, Tojo?"

"Pretty far afield," I said.

"I'm not blind, Tojo," she said. "I've seen what we've been toting around with us for the past two weeks. *How* far afield?"

"Very far," I answered.

"Who is he taking?"

"A bunch of people. Anyone he thinks can pull their weight with the show."

"What about Queenie and me, then? Why isn't he taking us?"

"You'll have to ask *him*, Alma."

She nodded, and we sat in silence for a few minutes. Then I heard footsteps approaching, and a moment later Thaddeus entered the tent.

"Tojo, where the hell have you been?" he said. "I still have to see—"

He broke off in midsentence when he saw Alma.

"Hello, Thaddeus," she said.

"I didn't know you were here," he said uncomfortably.

"I was just saying goodbye to Tojo. I guess I'll be saying goodbye to most of my friends, won't I?"

"Not to your best one. You belong with her, and she belongs here."

"But why, Thaddeus?"

"You've been a stripper long enough."

"I don't understand," she said.

"I've got enough strippers, and Romany is killing the meat show. Starting tomorrow, you and Queenie are running the games, unless you can convince him you're enough of an actress to put you in the specialty tent. But whatever he does, you're not going to be pawed by anyone from now on, unless you want to be."

"But we could work *your* games."

He shook his head. "I'm not taking anyone with any ties here. You've got Queenie, and Queenie's got family."

"That's not the reason," she said.

"All right. You couldn't earn your keep."

"Are you taking Priscilla?"

"Yes."

"Then that's not the reason either."

"It's over," he said, looking into her eyes. "It's my fault, and I'll take the blame for it—but that doesn't alter the fact of it."

"It doesn't have to be," she said without conviction.

"I thought we settled that a couple of nights ago. Queenie loves you. I'm not going to fight her to get you back."

"I wouldn't let it happen," she said firmly.

He sighed deeply. "You couldn't stop it from happening, Alma. All my life I've wanted what people told me I couldn't have. Why the hell do you think I'm going with Mr. Ahasuerus?"

"But—"

"It's settled," he said sharply. Then he smiled. "You're making it very difficult for me to be noble."

She looked at him for a long moment.

"All right, Thaddeus," she said. "If that's the way it has to be."

"That's the way it is," he answered.

She ran a hand through her hair, took a deep breath, and tried to change the subject.

"Does Mr. Romany know how to run a carnival?"

"Not very well," admitted Thaddeus. "He had a pretty bush-league operation when we found him. Of course, he was trying not to attract attention then, but just the same I think you'll have to help him in the beginning." He, too, seemed relieved by the change in subject, and addressed it eagerly. "I bought my rides back with the money we made off the aliens. The son of a bitch I sold them to held 'em for two weeks and sold them back for twenty grand more than he paid; I wish I'd have known I was going to need them again. Anyway, you'll have the rides and you'll keep most of the games, and of course Romany will have six or seven groups of aliens through here every year, so I imagine you'll make out okay. It's not as if he's shelling out a goddamned cent for the thing."

"What do *you* get out of this deal, Thaddeus?" asked Alma.

"The stars," he said with just a touch of irony.

She looked at him for a long time, a bittersweet expression on her face.

"You're never coming back, are you?" she said at last. It was not really a question.

"There are an awful lot of sheep up there waiting to be fleeced," he replied. It was not really an answer, but it served as one.

She stood up and extended her hand to him. "Good luck, Thaddeus. I'll look up every night and try to imagine where you are."

He took her hand awkwardly. "Good luck to you too, Alma."

Then she was out of the Hothouse and walking rapidly back to her trailer.

"How many more have I got to see on that list?" asked Thaddeus wearily.

I pulled it out and looked at it. "Seven." I paused. "Unless you've added someone."

"Like who?"

I found I didn't have the courage to tell him.

"Like Big Alvin," I said lamely.

He shook his head. "Who needs a roughie on a tour like this?"

"But what about Gloria?" I asked.

"I've already talked to her. I told her I wasn't taking anyone I couldn't use, and that she could come along or stay behind as she pleased, but Alvin stayed."

"And?"

"She's coming. It'll work out just as well for Alvin. He could have wasted another five years before he figured out that all she cares about is her dancing." He yawned. "Jesus, I'm tired. I was up all day yesterday working this out with Mr. Ahasuerus, and then I spent half the night on his shuttlecraft's radio selling his company on the idea of a traveling carnival, and the whole time I had to make sure Romany didn't throw any monkey wrenches into the deal, and I've spent most of today convincing a bunch of con men that I'm not trying to pull the biggest con of all."

He looked out the window and saw Stogie walking his little pet schnauzer on the snow.

"I don't know what the hell we're going to do about that dog," he said. Then he shrugged. "What the hell. If we can carry leopards and a lion and a bear, I suppose the old bastard can take along a ten-pound dog."

He opened the door and shouted, "Hey, Stogie—come over to my trailer! I've got to talk to you about something."

I considered going back to the Dancer's trailer to spend a final evening with my friends, but I knew that Monk and Diggs would be talking excitedly about their future, and the future wasn't something that appealed to me at that moment. So I sat in the Hothouse, totally alone, and realized that being totally alone was something I was going to have to get used to again.

16.

The activity started the next morning, and got a little frenzied as the day wore on.

Mr. Romany and the Rigger spent a few hours dividing up the games, arguing about who got which. Monk decided that he had no confidence in Mr. Ahasuerus' ability to get the proper food for his animals, and drove his bus—aliens and all—into a nearby town to pick up two hundred pounds of meat from a rather surprised butcher shop. One of the trucks had to be unloaded when it was discovered that the strippers' costumes, which were going with Thaddeus, had been packed under the specialty tent, which was staying with Mr. Romany. Big Alvin got drunk and had to be restrained when he started breaking windows in a number of vans and trailers. Stogie's schnauzer got loose and didn't turn up again for almost two hours.

But finally, by late afternoon, all was in readiness, and Thaddeus announced that his division of *The Ahasuerus and Flint Traveling Carnival and Sideshow* would be ready to move out in ten minutes. He then rounded up a number of men from Romany's division to accompany him so they could drive the vehicles back after his group had left.

I had spent most of the day alone in the trailer, trying to work up the courage to ask Thaddeus to take me with him. Once or twice I got as far as the door, but then I remembered that he wouldn't even take Big Alvin along, and I knew there was no way I could convince him that I could earn my keep. So I stayed where I was, and counted down the hours and the minutes.

I even considered going over to Monk's bus and throwing myself on Mr. Ahasuerus' mercy, but I knew he had more important things on his mind than the future of an ugly little hunchback who had trouble speaking, and I couldn't bring myself to face the finality of a negative answer. I guess deep down I thought that as long as he didn't officially turn me down, there was always the chance that he might change his mind at the last minute. I wondered what odds the Rigger would give on it.

The drive to the shuttlecraft took about forty minutes. When I felt us come to a halt I looked out the window and saw that we were in a large clearing, surrounded by a snow-covered forest. The wind was blowing the finely powdered snow through the air, and even though we were less than fifty yards away I couldn't make out any of the huge craft's features. It looked more like a grounded submarine than anything else I could think of.

I saw the aliens, most of them wearing coats and wrapped up in blankets, begin the short trek to the ship, and then Monk started unloading and moving his animals. I wiped the fog off the window, hoping for a last look at Diggs and the Dancer, when I felt a sudden cold draft.

Thaddeus was standing in the doorway, hands on hips, looking mildly irritated.

"Well?" he said.

"Well what?"

"Aren't you packed yet?"

"I thought I'd keep on living in the trailer," I said. "Unless you've given it to someone else, that is."

"What the hell are you talking about? You're coming with us."

"Me?" I exclaimed.

He snorted. "You see anyone else in here?"

"But . . . but what can I do? You said everyone has to earn his way."

"Everyone will," Thaddeus assured me. "*Especially* you."

"I don't understand."

"I'm going to be too damned busy running this carnival to do anything else. I mean, Mr. Ahasuerus is a nice guy and all, but you can fill a library's worth of books with what he doesn't know about operating a business." He paused. "Well, how about it?"

"How about what?" I asked.

"You've always wanted to be a barker, haven't you?"

"Yes, but . . ." I started tripping on my tongue again and couldn't get the words out.

"Mr. Ahasuerus tells me that a hell of a lot of the worlds we're going to visit communicate by telepathy.

So," he said with a smile, "unless you stammer when you think, you've got yourself a job."

"Do you really mean it, Thaddeus?" I managed to say.

"Would I lie to you, you ugly little dwarf?" he said gently.

It took me less than a minute to fill a suitcase with all of my worldly belongings. Then I put on my coat and followed him through the cold Vermont snow to the waiting spacecraft.

MIKE RESNICK was born in Chicago in 1942, attended the University of Chicago (where, in the process of researching his first adventure novel, he earned three letters on the fencing team and was nationally ranked for a brief period), and married his wife, Carol, in 1961. They have one daughter, Laura.

From the time he was 22, Mike has made his living as a professional writer. He and Carol have also been very active at science fiction conventions, where Mike is a frequent speaker and Carol's stunning costumes have swept numerous awards at masquerade competitions.

Mike and Carol were among the leading breeders and exhibitors of show collies during the 1970s, a hobby which led them to move to Cincinnati and purchase a boarding and grooming kennel.

Mike has received several awards for his short stories and an award for a nonfiction book for teenagers. His first love, though, remains science fiction, and his excellent science fiction novels, THE SOUL EATER, BIRTHRIGHT: THE BOOK OF MAN, and WALPURGIS III, are also available in Signet editions.